Stories to Share with My Partner
Book 7

A Northport Booksellers Publication

José F. Nodar

Stories to Share with My Partner Book 7 / José F. Nodar

ISBN: 978-1-7637054-2-5 - Paperback

ISBN: 978-1-7637054-3-2 - E-Book

ISBN: 978-0-9756618-5-7 - Audiobook

Table of Contents

Dedication...1

Life Just Got Better 2

Honoured The Fallen 6

Chicken Schnitzel 14

Farewell..18

Freddie Jenkins Bible Salesman...........................21

The Time Café 26

The Midnight Conference......................................29

Goal For The Day..35

Performance Artist 42

Booting Up History 48

Survival 55

Magical Chaos..58

Spaced Out..62

Shock Therapy..70

The Key 75

Personal Ad 81

Flirt...83

The Gazebo 86

Reviews 91

Perfect Job 96

Murder Or Divorce...104

Second Chance For Romance 108

G'day 113

Cheesecake 118

Zugzwang Love Triangle 124

Good Change 131

The Plot Twist 140

Nyc Newest Police Department 150

In Bitter Creek No One Is Innocent 158

A Boy And His Koala 164

The Time Traveller's Loopy Tale 171

Two Old Crows 173

The Vanishing Bride 178

About the Author 192

Dedication

Foremost, to my wife Miriam, who is always my muse, my inspiration, and has made everything wonderful in my life.

Also, to my daughter Anna, and stepdaughters Eliza-beth and Allison, who often give their encouragement and love.

To my grandchildren Rachel and David, and my step-granddaughter Andrea, who have contributed to my life intensively without them even knowing it.

To my friends of many years and most recent ones who have tolerated me discussing my ideas too many times at best.

To the talented professionals who have used that talent to make me look good on these pages through their copyediting and proofreading, book cover design, and narration of the audiobook. I am in your debt.

Finally, to my fellow authors, and those who have supported me through my journey as an author. I thank you for your help.

Life Just Got Better

Angus served Jimmy Armstrong a schooner of beer and left him alone. Jimmy just wanted to be by himself. To sit at the pub stool, mind his own business and take care of things how he wanted to.

Just as he was about to reach for his beer, a big, bad, burly looking fellow came along, hit the little guy on the shoulder, and drank his beer.

Jimmy couldn't help himself. He started sobbing loudly, desperately. That was his last straw.

The big, burly bully gave Jimmy an odd look and said, "Don't be like that, you plump wimp! Crying for a beer!"

Jimmy dropped his head into his hands. "My whole day has been miserable and here you come and take my last beer."

The man rolled his eyes. "Yeah, well, tough it out, buddy. Size matters."

"You don't understand! My life has just been a total mess!"

For the first time in a longtime, the big burly bully felt an ounce of sympathy for his fellow humankind. He looked at Jimmy and asked, "What's your name?"

"Jimmy Armstrong." Jimmy extended his hand.

The bully shook his head. "I am not making friends here, buddy; just wanted to know your name."

"OK, I just thought I care since you asked and thought you might be interested why I was having a beer here."

"No, I am not interested, but you seem determined to tell me." The big, burly bully sighed. "So, I will give you a chance to tell me your sad story."

"Well then, listen up." Jimmy straightened and cleared his throat. "This morning my wife left me; she cleared our account."

"Yes, that is tough. I had a friend that happened to. So?"

"It gets better. I found the house empty. She took all the furniture with her, too. Everything!"

"OK, that sucks," agreed the big, bad, burly guy.

"Oh, it gets even better. My boss called me into the office this morning and made me redundant. I now have no job to pay off the mortgage on an empty house!"

"Bummer," was all big bag burly guy said. He rubbed at his chest, which was tightening up a bit.

"I didn't want to live anymore, so I put myself on a railway track and hoped for a quick ending."

"And?"

"No train came!"

"Jimmy, you seem to be on a bad streak, buddy," said a big, bad, burly guy, almost sounding compassionate.

"Then I wanted to hang myself, so I went home and grabbed some rope. I tied it to the ceiling, stood on the kitchen counter, wrapped it around my neck and jumped, but the rope ripped, and I just tumbled onto the kitchen floor!"

The big, bad, burly guy rubbed his ever-increasingly tightening chest and said, "Luck is not on your side today, is it, Jimmy?"

"It appears so. Then I looked for a quick way and went and bought a gun. Returned home. Sat on the lounge floor and I pulled the trigger and the darn thing jams!"

"Wow. Then what?" The bully was finding himself interested despite himself.

"I decided on another approach, and I went to my local hardware store, Bunnings—the one over Narellan. You know which one I am talking about?"

"Yes, I do." His chest was so tight now. He clutched it hard this time.

Jimmy shook his head, suddenly exhausted. "With my few last dollars I bought myself a beer, poured all the rat poison I'd bought at Bunnings into it... and just when I was about to drink it, you walk in and drank it away!"

The big, bad, burly bully reached over to Jimmy but simply fell to the pub's floor.

Dead.

Jimmy bent over and checked the guy's pulse. Once he'd realised the big, bad burly guy was no longer amongst the living, he reached into his back pocket and pulled out the wallet. He removed several 100 dollar notes and called to Angus to fetch an ambulance.

When the ambulance arrived and took the lifeless body of the big, bad, burly bully away, Jimmy was no longer sad. Because now, with a couple thousand dollars in his pocket, life just got better.

Honoured The Fallen

Anya's knuckles bled white against the cold metal of the console; her desperate commands swallowed by the relentless groan of the dying engines. Crimson alarms pulsed, an infernal heartbeat against the backdrop of the roaring atmosphere. Below, the alien world loomed, a tapestry of swirling greens and blues woven through with jagged obsidian veins, speeding closer with every second. Fear, sharp, and suffocating, clawed at her throat, but a deeper instinct thrummed beneath it—survival.

"Anya, what are the power levels on the left thrusters? Can you increase them? Compensate? I need the power now!" the captain commanded.

"I am punching all the codes, Captain. It's working as best as it can, but the power isn't budging. It's at max propulsion."

Cursing the unyielding code that mocked her efforts, Anya slammed her fist against the console. Sparks danced, mimicking the tears stinging her eyes. Was this it? The bitter culmination of their audacious mission, reduced to a fiery epitaph on this unforgiving world?

She glanced at Kai, her copilot; a grim acceptance replaced his usual unflappable demeanour. His hand met hers in a silent testament to their shared journey, one destined to end prematurely.

Suddenly, they plunged into the planet.

The crash was over in minutes, leaving behind a chilling silence as thick as the smoke that billowed from the smouldering wreckage. Dust motes danced in the golden light of the setting sun, catching on the faces of the stunned survivors as they emerged from their hiding places. Among them was Kai. He'd made it with a handful of others.

Her gaze darted across the scene, searching for more familiar faces, a reassuring sign of life amidst the debris.

The air reeked of burnt metal and singed earth, and Anya knew she needed to act quickly.

With a deep breath, Anya reached to make sure the tattered book was still inside her satchel.

As the survivors gathered around, Anya shouted: "Everyone quickly. Run towards those trees and take cover in case the ship explodes."

It was a gamble, but it was their only hope. Fear pulsed through her veins, yet determination hardened her voice.

"Go faster, go faster," knowing the explosion was going to happen at any moment.

Anya turned and watched as the crackling flames continue to engulf the ship and then...

It blew up, but Anya and her comrades were safe in the woods.

Nine women.

Their faces smudged with soot and etched with exhaustion, their ragged cloaks billowing like smoke—surged forward. One stumbled, a young girl barely a woman, and a broad-shouldered engineer by the looks of the tarred uniform scooped her up, carrying her like a precious bundle. Her own limp hinted at a hidden injury, but she pressed on, driven by the primal urge to survive.

Beside them, five men stood, their eyes wild with a mix of terror and fierce defiance. Among them was Kai. He was Anya's closest friend, and she felt a surge of relief as he urged everyone to go in deeper into the forest, leading the group to safety. His usually gentle face was contorted with grim determination as he clutched a medic's box. How he'd had a mind to retrieve it was beyond her. Kai glanced back, their eyes meeting for a fleeting moment, and Anya saw the silent plea for forgiveness, the unspoken acceptance of their uncertain fate.

Then they disappeared into the forest, and they were gone.

They had somehow survived the crash, but many of their comrades had not. This handful of women and men now needed to find shelter, water, and food on a planet not in their star charts.

Anya reached the nine women and five men, their faces smudged with soot and etched with the stark horror of the past day, stood scattered around the edge of the forest. Tears, silent and glistening, snaked down Anya's cheeks as she touched Kai's shoulder. His eyes were vacant, staring into a void only he could see.

Grief threatened to drown them, to steal their will to survive, but something flickered within Anya. A spark, ignited by the shared breath in their lungs; they had survived, and with that survival came a duty to honour those who had not.

This planet was not on their star charts.

They did not know what to expect.

Anya watched her team and commanded: "We need to go back and see what we can salvage, if anything, from the ship. No time to waste. Look around and pickup anything of value you can carry. Return here and we will set up a perimeter."

Returning to the smouldering wreckage, they began salvaging what they could. They gathered as many tools as possible and rations that had survived the fire. "Pick up anything of value. We will sort it out later once we setup camp," exclaimed Anya.

Of course, water was their immediate concern and Elara, ever the resourceful one, pointed towards a distant grove of trees, their emerald leaves shimmering in the alien sunlight.

"There should be water there," her voice was hoarse but resolute. "Water might gather there."

"Good spotting, Elara," shouted Anya. "You might be right. There may be water there. Let us go, everyone; gather what you can that will hold water. Now!"

And so, they headed towards the spot Elara had pointed.

With each step, Anya thought of the new responsibility that been thrust upon her. She was a pilot, not a captain, but since he hadn't survived, she was the only remaining semblance of command.

Anya was used to the stars, the only familiar constant in this alien landscape, as she guided her companions through the uncharted terrain.

The rustle of unseen creatures, the chilling howl of wind through twisted canyons, punctuated the trek and hunger gnawed at their bellies while fear of the unknown mounted, but they pressed on, pushed on by Anya and driven by a shared flicker of hope.

A few hours later, Kai pointed toward a low-lying valley. Amongst: Amongst the crimson vegetation, a blue ribbon shimmered. A river surrounded by the emerald leaves of the trees Elara had seen.

Finally, they found the precious lifeline: water.

"Kai, run a quick analysis to make sure it is safe to drink," Anya said.

Kai grabbed some small containers out of his medic kit and scooped up some of the flowing water. A minute later, he smiled and turned to his teammates. "It is safe to drink."

The group collapsed on the bank of the river and, using their hands, they cupped the cool water in their chapped hands. It tasted unlike anything they had tasted before. It was metallic and tangy, but it was water. The source of life itself.

In the days that followed, they learned to observe the alien sky, to decipher when the rough winds will blow, and the rains will come. They could sense the changing seasons, well, they call it season, as they made their new home.

They discovered which plants were edible and which to stay away from. Kai documented their finds, sketching the curious flora and fauna, meticulously recording their journey through the days using the notebooks salvaged from the wreckage.

They saw strange carnivores whose meats they ate and whose skins they used to make clothing.

Farming also was something the group started experimenting with and a watermelon type of fruit like was their first success.

Several months have passed and as they huddled around a crackling fire one night, Elara's voice broke the silence. "We will build a city here," she said.

Anya looked around at the faces. The quiet courage burning in their eyes.

Nine women and five men.

Anya knew Elara was right.

They were the new seeds that would be planted on this alien soil of this unknown world.

They would build a new home, a human home, a testament to the unyielding human spirit.

By doing this, they would honour the fallen by living, by thriving, and by whispering their stories to the next generations.

Their survival was not just a triumph against the crash; it was a pledge to the future.

Chicken Schnitzel

The battlefield was set, stretching out in stark black and white across the table. Morning light slanted through the window, casting long shadows over the two armies locked in silent formation. The air was thick with tension, though no weapons clashed, nor soldiers cried out in battle.

In the chair at one end of the battlefield sat a seasoned warrior, his hair as grey as the marble pieces before him. Opposite him, a junior commander, leaned forward, her eyes sparkling with determination.

José surveyed the terrain, his eyes squinting with practiced scrutiny. His hand hovered over the lines of pawns; foot soldiers prepared to sacrifice themselves for his cause. Across the board, his granddaughter, gripping her queen with determination, shifted in her seat, ready for the clash.

"Your move, little general," José grumbled, his voice gravelly yet warm. He folded his hands and waited, like a seasoned tactician confident in his strategy.

She glanced at her pieces, a myriad of possibilities whirling in her mind. Her brows furrowed, and then, with a sharp intake of breath, she sent her knight galloping forward.

The L-shaped path swept the wooden steed across the board, ready to spring into the enemy's ranks.

"Hmm," the old warrior murmured, eyes glinting. "So, you advance the cavalry first. Bold." He moved a bishop with the precision of a swordsman wielding his blade. The ivory-robed cleric slid diagonally, threatening her advancing knight. "But you've left your flank exposed."

She clenched her teeth but did not back down. Her pawns surged forward, bravely marching to meet the enemy head-on. "Then I'll guard it with my foot soldiers," she declared, her voice steady, betraying none of the butterflies that churned in her stomach.

For every move she made, her grandfather countered with a seasoned touch. His rook stormed across the board like a chariot, capturing a pawn in a sweeping motion. Yet, she stood resolutely, her eyes fixed on the centre. She had learned from him the art of patience and cunning. This was not a game of brute force; it was a dance of wits.

Time slowed as the battle raged on. Knights leapt over pawns, bishops sliced through lines, and rooks swept across the field like rolling thunder. She narrowed her focus, blocking out the world beyond the board. It was only her and her grandfather now, locked in a silent duel of minds.

Suddenly, she saw it—a weakness in his defences. A glimmer of an opportunity. Her heart pounded as she moved her queen forward, a decisive lunge towards the enemy's king. The queen stood tall and proud, facing her adversary with unwavering resolve.

José grunted, a smile curling the corners of his mouth. "So, the queen charges into battle." He moved a pawn, attempting to shield his king from the oncoming threat.

Her hands trembled in anticipation, but she did not falter. She directed her rook forward, pinning his remaining bishop in place. His eyes widened ever so slightly; she had forced his hand. The battlefield had shifted in her favour.

With a slow, deliberate motion, she advanced her queen once more. "Check," she said, her voice a whisper on the edge of anticipation.

His eyes met hers, twinkling with a mixture of pride and the thrill of battle. He studied the board, his fingers stroking his chin thoughtfully. With a heavy sigh, he tipped his king over, the soft clatter echoing like the final toll of a distant bell.

"Well played," he said, his voice thick with admiration. "You've won this time."

She beamed, her heart swelling with victory. The battle was over, the battlefield quiet. Pieces lay scattered, some fallen, some still standing proudly in their places. She had won the day, not through force, but through strategy and patience.

As they set the pieces back in their original positions, the grandfather leaned over and whispered, "But remember, the war is far from over. I'll be back for another match."

She grinned, a glint of future battles already shining in her eyes. "I'll be ready, Granddad."

"I bet you will be," he said, grabbing her hand before leading her into the kitchen where the aromas of lunch prepared by his wife were enveloping the room.

"Let's see what Nanna has made for lunch."

"Chicken schnitzel, I hope," was her answer.

Farewell

As Jerry sat down at the park bench, unpacking his lunch, he felt a sense of calm. The sun was shining, and his sandwich looked majestic. Thick slices of turkey, perfectly arranged lettuce, and a dollop of mayo that whispered, "you deserve this." But as Jerry prepared to take his first bite, he heard a familiar buzz.

A fly.

Not just any fly. A persistent, uninvited guest who had decided that Jerry's sandwich was the culinary event of the day. The fly zoomed past his face, made a beeline for the sandwich, and hovered there like a food critic deciding how many stars to award his meal.

"Really?" Jerry muttered. "Of all the places to be, you pick here. During lunch?"

The fly ignored him, continuing its dizzying loops around the sandwich. Jerry waved his hand, trying to shoo it away, but the fly took this as a challenge. It swooped and swerved; dodging Jerry's attempts like a tiny, winged ninja.

"Come on, buddy, I don't have time for this!" Jerry pleaded. "I'm on a break! I've got exactly 25 minutes to enjoy this sandwich, and you are seriously cramping my vibe!"

The fly, of course, didn't care. It circled Jerry's head, now toying with him like it had some personal vendetta. Jerry flailed his arms, looking like he was performing an interpretive dance for the park pigeons, who watched, clearly unimpressed.

"Alright, fine. I see how it is," Jerry said, dropping his sandwich back into its wrapper. "You win. Let's just talk this out, okay?"

The fly landed on the bench, giving Jerry what he imagined was a smug look. Jerry sighed.

"Listen, I get it. You're living your best life. You have fly family responsibilities I don't understand. Little fly kids, a mortgage on a decaying banana peel. But can't a man eat lunch in peace?"

He paused, feeling absurd for reasoning with a fly. And then, as if to mock him one last time, the fly took off, buzzing lazily away. Just like that. Gone.

Jerry blinked. "Wait... that's it? You're leaving? After all that?"

He watched the fly disappear into the distance and shook his head in disbelief. "Well, thanks for nothing. Farewell," he muttered to himself.

He looked down at his sandwich. Still perfect. He picked it up, finally ready to take that first bite, and then he heard the familiar buzz.

"Not farewell?!"

Freddie Jenkins Bible Salesman

The Unified Church of God in Northport NSW needed a new roof, so Reverend Johnson thought that a campaign to sell bibles to the good people of Northport and surrounds would be a terrific way to raise money and spread the word of God.

Reverend Johnson calculated that the more bibles his congregation sold then the more funds would be for the new roof since, as more bibles were printed, the cost per bible would be lower. So, he did a quick calculation. If each adult in his congregation sold 1,000 bibles at $50 each and the cost per bible was $5, the church would have a profit of $45. And this would be more than enough to cover the new roof.

He placed the order and, once the bibles arrived, he set out to instruct the congregation on how to sell the book. "Just offer to the good people of Northport and surrounds the opportunity to bring God into their home," is what the reverend said.

On the morning of the big day, Reverend Johnson handed each adult member of the congregation their quota of five hundred bibles. The last person was Freddie Jenkins.

Now Freddie Jenkins was a nice guy, always polite, and had a heart of gold. But he had one slight problem: Freddie was extremely shy.

Freddie Jenkins was as shy as they came. He often walked with his head slightly down, hands stuffed deep into his pockets, as if he were trying to shrink into himself and disappear. He rarely made eye contact, preferring to stare at his shoes while shuffling along. His voice, when he could manage to use it, was soft and quiet, almost like a whisper, as if every word cost him a great deal of effort to push out.

Social situations made Freddie's heart race; his palms would sweat, and his mouth would go dry. The idea of approaching a stranger made his stomach twist into knots. Whenever he found himself in a conversation, he fiddled with the hem of his shirt or scratched the back of his neck; his nervousness on full display.

Despite all this, when the bible-selling fundraiser came around, Freddie could not say no. Not because he was brave or confident, but simply because he was too shy to refuse. So, with a timid nod and a slight tremor in his hands, he took the stack of bibles, ready to do what everyone else thought he could not.

While everyone was excited, Freddie was not. The rest of the young parishioners chuckled and whispered among themselves, betting on who would sell the most bibles. No one thought Freddie stood a chance.

The reverend handed out the bibles to Freddie, with his usual cheery grin, who took his pile. "Thank you, Reverend," he said.

The Reverend gave him a supportive pat on the back and muttered a quiet prayer under his breath.

With his list of streets to canvas, Freddie walked down the first street. He just did not know how he was going to do this—and then, as if a light bulb had gone in his head, he thought of an idea.

The first house Freddie approached belonged to old Ms Hastings, a woman notorious for her icy demeanour and sharp tongue. Freddie stepped up to the door, knocked and waited. The door creaked open.

"Yes? What do you want?" Ms Hastings barked.

"I-I-I'm se-se-se-selling b-b-b-bibles," Freddie stammered, holding up the book.

Ms Hastings raised an eyebrow and crossed her arms, clearly ready to shut the door.

Freddie took another deep breath and continued, "W-w-would you li-li-like to b-b-buy one or w-w-would you like me to re-re-re-read it to you?"

There was a moment of silence. Ms Hastings stared at him, eyes wide in disbelief. Then, before she knew what was happening, she dug into her purse and shoved a crumpled $50 note into Freddie's hand. "Here, just... I will take it," she muttered, snatching the bible and slamming the door shut.

Freddie blinked in surprise and grinned. One down, hundreds to go!

By the end of the day, Freddie had visited every house on his list and sold all his bibles.

Back at the church, the parishioners gathered around the table, stacking their sales sheets and counting their earnings. When Freddie walked in, his arms full of money and not a single bible left in his basket, everyone's jaws dropped.

"Well, I'll be..." Reverend Johnson gasped. "Freddie, you sold all of them?"

Freddie blushed and nodded. "Yes, Reverend."

So, the reverend finally sat him down and said, "Okay, Freddie, spill it. How on earth did you sell so many bibles?"

Freddie leaned in, serious, and said, "Well, it is simple. I knock on the door, and when they answered, I said, 'W-w-w-would you L-like to b-buy a b-b-bible, or sh-should I s-s-sit down and r-r-read it to you c-c-c-cover to c-c-c-cover?'

From that day on, Freddie was known as the church's top bible salesman.

And the secret to his success?

Sometimes, it wasn't how you said it; it was how long you took to say it.

The Time Café

The small town of Ticktock, New South Wales, had a café called The Time Café. The café was infamous not for its coffee but for its clocks. More specifically, its erratic sense of time.

Inside the café, time simply refused to behave. The moment you walked through the door, you could age backward, forward, or just sideways. On one wall, a grandfather clock ticked insistently, but if you stared at it too long, it would shout, "Hurry up!" and fling a scone in your direction. Nobody could explain why, but the scones were always perfectly warm.

Miriam, the café owner, insisted it wasn't her fault. "I bought this place off a wizard on clearance," she said, waving a spatula at the customers. "He said the clocks would 'add flavour.' I assumed he meant ambiance, not this freaking chaos!"

On any given day, you'd find a bizarre mix of patrons. At table three, a toddler was lecturing her bemused mother on quantum physics because she'd accidentally aged 20 years during breakfast. Nearby, two grey-haired men were arm-wrestling, but one of them was secretly twelve and kept cheating by rewinding his biceps strength.

Barry, the local postal worker, popped in daily for an espresso. "Just one cup," he'd said, "or I'll be late for my route." But thanks to the café's quirky time loops, Barry often delivered letters before they were written, leading to a town-wide ban on sending love notes.

One fateful morning, a tourist named Kevin strolled in, oblivious to the chaos. He ordered a croissant and sat by the window. Within minutes, Kevin found himself locked in an argument with his future self over whether he should move to Bali or marry his girlfriend. "But Bali has beaches!" Kevin shouted.

"Yes, but you hate sand!" Future Kevin countered.

"Do not!"

"You absolutely do, mate. You made a PowerPoint presentation about it last year."

Meanwhile, Miriam sighed behind the counter as she poured a latte that somehow turned into a cappuccino halfway through. "Time waits for no one," she muttered. Then she glanced at the wall clock, which read 13 o'clock. "In here, time's an absolute jerk," she mumbled to herself.

By the end of the day, Kevin left the café with a half-eaten croissant and a life plan, while the grandfather clock hummed a lullaby, content with another chaotic shift. Miriam just prayed the wizard wouldn't return for his scones.

The Midnight Conference

The Art Gallery of Northport, New South Wales, was the pride of the town. By day, its halls buzzed with visitors marvelling at masterpieces from across centuries. But by night, extraordinary things happened that no one would even imagine.

As the last staff member locked the doors and dusk blanketed the town, the paintings stirred.

Colours rippled, figures stretched, and whispers turned into full conversations as the painted subjects began their nightly ritual of coming alive.

The vibrant subjects of Ariadne by Arthur Streeton were the first to move. The Greek goddess, her draped gown flowing as if caught in a real breeze, stepped from her canvas. She yawned. "It's been centuries, but I still hate lying in that pose all day," she muttered.

"Join the club," said the bushranger from Tom Roberts' Bailed Up. He adjusted his bandana and tipped his hat at Ariadne. "Though at least I get to sit on a horse."

Nearby, Margaret Preston's Flapper strutted down from her frame, her bright modernist dress swishing dramatically. "Horse or not, darling, try holding still with this kind of energy bottled up all day." She twirled on her heels, added, "Anyway, where's everyone else?"

The other paintings joined them. The Bohemian, with his melancholy eyes and cigarette dangling precariously from his lips, shuffled out reluctantly. The stately figures from The Visit of the Queen of Sheba to King Solomon sauntered in, their ancient robes flowing magnificently.

Last to emerge were the stormy figures from J. M. W. Turner's Keelmen Heaving in Coals by Moonlight. They were a dramatic lot, trailing water and flickering light wherever they went. "Could we not discuss something cheery for once?" grumbled one sailor, wringing out his cap.

As the clock struck midnight, the gallery hummed with activity. The figures gathered in the Grand Hall, sitting on marble steps and perching on pedestals.

"So, what's tonight's topic?" asked the bushranger, polishing his revolver. He had a sly glint in his eye, clearly enjoying the gatherings more than he let on.

"Art!" declared the Queen of Sheba. "Specifically, the point of art. Is it to evoke emotion? To tell a story? Or simply to decorate walls?"

Ariadne rolled her eyes. "Typical. It's always 'art this' or 'art that.' How about we debate something real, like whether Turner overuses the colour grey?"

Turner's sailors gasped in indignation. One called out, "I'll have you know it's muted lavender, not grey!"

The Flapper, with a smirk, stepped forward. "Darling, I think you're both missing the point. Art is about making a statement. Look at me—I'm bold, modern, and fabulous."

"But do you stand the test of time?" retorted the bushranger. "You're trendy now, but what happens when the next big thing comes along? I'm history."

The debate escalated. The Queen of Sheba argued for the grandeur of storytelling, while The Bohemian insisted art was for introspection. The Turner sailors lamented how people overlooked the technical precision of their moonlit water, and Ariadne debated whether art should be appreciated for its beauty alone.

Amid the lively arguments, a low creak echoed through the gallery. The figures froze, their painted skin seeming to ripple with unease.

From the darkened corner of the hall emerged a shadowy figure—a sculpture of The Thinker, who usually sat brooding in a distant gallery. He walked stiffly, his bronze limbs groaning as if they hadn't moved in centuries.

The Flapper quipped, "Well, well, if it isn't the strong and silent type. Come to share your opinion?"

The Thinker raised his head slowly. "I've listened to your debates for decades," he said in a gravelly voice. "And I must say, your chatter grows tiresome."

The group exchanged uneasy glances. The Thinker rarely spoke, and when he did, it was never to praise.

"Art is neither emotion nor story," he continued. "It reflects humanity's endless struggle to understand itself. It is profound. It is painful. It is..."

"Boring," interrupted the bushranger. "Get off your pedestal, mate."

The group burst into laughter, and even the solemn Thinker cracked a small smile. The tension melted as the figures resumed their usual banter, the heaviness of the sculpture's words dissipating into the warm glow of camaraderie.

As the night wore on, the paintings felt the familiar tug of dawn. Their colours dimmed slightly; their movements grew sluggish. Ariadne stretched one last time before climbing back into her canvas. "Same time tomorrow, then?"

"Of course," said the Queen of Sheba. "The debate isn't over."

"Never is," muttered The Bohemian, dragging his chair back into his frame.

The Flapper blew a kiss to the group. "Don't forget—art is fashion, darlings. Never forget!"

The Turner sailors returned to their stormy scene, their moonlit waves shimmering one last time before settling into stillness.

As the first rays of sunlight streamed into the gallery, silence returned. The paintings were once again just paintings, their vibrant personalities hidden beneath layers of paint. Guards opened the doors, and visitors wandered in, admiring the masterpieces with no idea of the nightly gatherings that brought them to life.

In one corner, a schoolgirl paused in front of The Thinker. She tilted her head. "Mum, why does he look like he's smiling?"

Her mother shrugged. "Maybe he's just happy to be here."

And somewhere deep within the bronze, The Thinker smiled again.

Goal For The Day

It was supposed to be an ordinary, and probably dull, school trip to the Northport Museum, but for a clumsy 15-year-old Joey Fitzpatrick, it was a disaster.

Joey had one simple goal for the day: to impress Madison Green, the girl he had been hopelessly crushing on since sixth grade, and hopefully steal a kiss. Madison, with her perfect ponytail and a cheerful coolness, was way out of his league, but Joey had convinced himself that this trip was his golden opportunity. Unfortunately, Joey's two left feet and knack for catastrophe had other plans.

The museum's pièce de résistance was the Golden Chalice of Karnak, a relic so ancient and precious that it was displayed in a glass case surrounded by velvet ropes and motion sensors. Their teacher, Ms. Carmichael, had warned them not to even breathe near it.

"Touch nothing," she said sternly, looking at her class.

Joey, busy trying to look nonchalant while stealing glances at Madison, nodded without listening. He had concocted a brilliant plan: he would impress Madison by casually standing near the chalice, looking intellectual and mysterious.

Maybe even throw in a witty historical fact he Googled earlier. He found out that the chalice might have been used in ancient rituals or for human sacrifices. He wasn't sure.

As the group entered the gallery housing the chalice, Joey stayed behind, pretending to study a placard. Madison was at the front, chatting with her friends, unaware of Joey's existence.

"Psst! Madison," he whispered, inching closer. She didn't hear him. Joey, determined not to lose his moment, tiptoed toward her, weaving through the crowd like an awkward ninja.

Unfortunately, Joey's coordination was as smooth as a two-legged giraffe on roller skates. As he leaned forward to tap Madison on the shoulder, he tripped over his own feet. Arms flailing like windmills, he stumbled forward, colliding with a volunteer guide carrying a tray of brochures.

The guide yelped as the brochures went flying. Joey, in a desperate bid to regain his balance, grabbed the nearest solid object. Of course it was—you guessed it—the velvet rope surrounding the chalice.

The rope stand toppled like a domino, its base hitting the glass case. A soft but ominous crack echoed through the room.

The entire group turned in unison. Ms. Carmichael gasped, Madison's jaw dropped, and the security guard standing nearby gasped.

"Don't move!" the guard barked, but Joey, in full panic mode, did the exact opposite.

To fix his mistake, Joey tried to prop the velvet rope back up. His elbow knocked into the case again, and this time, the crack expanded like a spiderweb. With a final crash, the glass shattered, and the Golden Chalice of Karnak tumbled out, landing in Joey's trembling hands.

For one glorious second, he was holding the most valuable artifact in the museum. Then, because Joey was Joey, it slipped through his sweaty fingers, bounced once on the floor, and rolled under a display of ancient pottery.

"JOSEPH FITZPATRICK!" Ms. Carmichael's voice could have shattered another glass case. The rest of the class stared in stunned silence, except for Madison, who was failing not to laugh.

The security guard stormed over, walkie-talkie in hand. "We've got a Code Chalice. Repeat, Code Chalice. Kid down."

Joey, still on all fours trying to retrieve the chalice, muttered, "I can fix this. I can fix this!" He reached for the chalice, but his backpack caught on the pottery display.

Before he could stop it, a row of ancient vases toppled over like bowling pins.

One by one, they shattered in a cascade of priceless ceramic shards.

As the chaos unfolded, Madison finally spoke. "Joey, what are you doing?"

Joey, face redder than a museum exit sign, stammered, "I-I just wanted to... um... say hi."

"Hi?" Madison repeated, raising an eyebrow. "You destroyed a 3,000-year-old artifact to say hi?"

Joey shrugged helplessly, still clutching a fragment of pottery. "Well, when you say it like that, it sounds bad."

Within minutes, the museum director arrived, flanked by more security guards and a woman in a power suit who looked like she lived for moments like this.

"Who is responsible for this... this disaster?" she demanded.

Ms. Carmichael pointed at Joey. "It's... him."

Joey tried to explain, but every word made it worse. "It was an accident! The chalice slipped, and then the vase thing—well, that wasn't really my fault because, you know, gravity—and..."

"Silence!" barked the woman in the power suit. "Do you have any idea what you've done? That chalice is worth more than your entire school!"

Joey gulped. "Well, not in this condition now..."

The guards dragged him to the lobby, where he was instructed to sit and "think about what he'd done." Meanwhile, the museum staff assessed the damage.

As Joey sat in shame, Madison approached him. "You really blew it, Fitzpatrick," she said, but there was a hint of amusement in her voice.

Joey buried his face in his hands. "I was just trying to... I don't know... impress you."

"By wrecking a museum?" Madison asked, sitting beside him. "Bold strategy."

Joey peeked through his fingers. "Did it work?"

Madison laughed. A real big laugh, not the mocking kind. "Well, it's definitely the most interesting thing that's happened on this school trip."

Just then, the museum director entered, looking oddly cheerful. "Joey Fitzpatrick, is it?"

Joey braced himself. "Yes, sir."

"Well, Joey, as much as it pains me to say this...you may have actually done us a favour."

Joey blinked. "I did?"

The director nodded. "While retrieving the chalice from under the pottery display, our team discovered an ancient scroll hidden inside the base of one of the vases. It's an artifact we didn't even know existed."

Ms. Carmichael, overhearing this, looked like she might faint. "So, he's not expelled?"

"Oh, he's banned from the museum for life," the director clarified. "But thanks to his clumsiness, we've uncovered something even more valuable."

Joey grinned sheepishly. "You're welcome?"

On the bus ride home, Joey expected to be the laughingstock of the school. But instead, he was a hero.

Even Madison seemed impressed, sitting next to him and chatting about how the museum staff were still buzzing about the discovery.

"Next time, maybe just ask me to hang out," she said and gave him a sweet kiss on his cheek.

Joey blushed and added, "Next time, I'll stay far away from ancient artifacts."

Madison laughed again, and for the first time, Joey felt like his disaster-prone ways weren't all bad. Sure, he'd been banned from the Northport Museum, but he'd also earned a kiss from Madison Green.

And that, in Joey's book, was priceless.

Performance Artist

Vince "The Chameleon" Hargrove considered himself a criminal mastermind, but lately, the universe had been treating him like an unpaid intern.

His goal: steal The Radiant Dawn, a $50 million painting at the Newport Museum of Art.

His problem: everything.

It wasn't Vince's first heist—he had a reputation for blending into places. Security guard? Nailed it. Caterer? Done it. Once, he'd pretended to be a janitor so convincingly that the museum actually gave him a paycheck.

But this time, the Newport Museum had upgraded its security system. It wasn't just a simple motion detector; it was a hyper-sensitive, AI-driven monstrosity that could tell the difference between a pigeon and a plastic bag in a windstorm.

Vince needed a plan.

So he started simple: he disguised himself as an art critic. He donned a black turtleneck, fake glasses, and carried a notebook filled with pretentious phrases like "the juxtaposition of light and despair speaks volumes." When the security guard at the entrance asked for his credentials, Vince handed him a business card that read, "Maxwell DeFontaine, Art Aficionado."

The guard squinted. "This looks like it was printed on a cereal box."

Vince laughed nervously. "Ah, yes, postmodern irony. It's a statement."

The guard waved him in, muttered something about "weirdos."

Once inside, Vince marvelled at his luck. He strolled confidently toward The Radiant Dawn, a 10-foot canvas surrounded by motion sensors, laser beams, and, for some reason, a potted fern.

Just as he reached the exhibit, a real art critic, complete with a monocle and the aura of someone who has never eaten a hot dog, approached him. "What do you think of the piece?" the critic asked, gesturing to a nearby sculpture of a giant nose titled Sniff of Eternity.

Vince panicked. "Ah, it's... sniff-tacular?"

The critic frowned. "You're not Maxwell DeFontaine. Maxwell's in Paris, and he hates noses."

Thwarted but undeterred, Vince devised a new plan: hacking the museum's security system. He borrowed a laptop from his tech-savvy nine-year-old nephew, Derek. The boy was nine, but already knew how to bypass parental controls on his tablet.

"I wrote you a program," Derek explained, handing over the laptop. "It's called Hackinator 3000. Just click the button that says, 'Do Crime.'"

Vince nodded solemnly. "You're a genius."

That night, Vince sat in a café across from the museum, had dinner and was enjoying a coffee when he opened the laptop and executed the program. The screen displayed a loading bar labelled Crime Progress: 97%.

"This is it," Vince whispered to himself.

Then the screen froze. A large pop up appeared: "Your session has expired. Please log in again."

Vince banged the table, spilling his coffee. He tried to reboot the program, only to find the laptop locked with a cartoon of a dancing cat and the message, "You should've bought the premium version!"

Mumbling to himself, Vince decided to go old-school, but how? Then, like a torch being ignited, an idea lit up in his mind: crawling through the air ducts. He devised his plan to wear his sleekest black outfit, covering a tuxedo.

Just in case, was his thought, and he added a ski mask and knee pads. He imagined himself as a shadow, silent and deadly, like a ninja.

Reality was less glamorous. The air ducts were narrower than expected, and Vince had become, well, a bit more rotund over the years and on top of that, he'd forgotten he was mildly claustrophobic. Halfway through, his phone buzzed.

"Not now, Derek," he hissed, accidentally activating speakerphone.

"Uncle Vince, I just wanted to say the museum has heat sensors too, so don't sweat."

"Too late," Vince groaned, as sweat dripped onto the metal below him.

Suddenly, the duct gave way, and Vince landed in a supply closet filled with brooms. Startled, he froze as two janitors walked in.

"Did you hear that?" one asked.

"Eh, probably just another raccoon."

Vince exhaled in relief.

Until one janitor poked him with a broom. "That's a big raccoon," he muttered, before running out screaming.

Vince's final plan had taken a turn, but he had prepared for that: he had his tuxedo! Removing the outer black outfit, he looked dapper in his tux, and he simply walked into the museum.

He sauntered in, his head held high. "Good evening, folks!" he greeted the guards, who eyed him suspiciously. "I'm here for a private viewing of The Radiant Dawn."

"Do you have an appointment?" one guard asked.

"No, but I have... charisma," Vince replied, winking.

They didn't laugh.

He walked toward the painting anyway, and they didn't follow or even watch him. He dodged lasers with a grace he didn't know he had. For a moment, it seemed like he might pull it off. Then, as he reached out to grab the painting, he tripped over the potted fern, setting off every alarm in the building.

In a blink, Vince found himself sitting in the security office, handcuffed and dejected. He couldn't help but laugh at his misfortune. A guard entered with a cup of coffee and handed it to him. "You're not very good at this, are you?"

Vince sighed. "Not today."

"You know, you've caused quite a stir. The museum's director wants to meet you. Finish the coffee and follow me."

Vince gulped the coffee and follow the security guard, and he was ushered into the museum director's office and promptly sat on the chair in front of the director's desk.

Holding a wallet in one hand and what looked like a driver's license in the other, the director said, "Mr Hargrove, is it? Your heist attempt has gone viral. People are flocking to the museum to see where you messed up. Our website ticket sales are through the roof! Look—"

The director put both the wallet and driver's license down and turned the monitor around to allow Vince to see.

Vince blinked. "What?"

"We'd like to propose a deal. We won't press charges if you agree to recreate your heist attempts for a live audience next month."

And so, without a moment's hesitation, Vince found himself a new career. Not as a thief, but as a performance artist.

The Radiant Dawn remained securely on the wall, and Vince, well, he became a star, proving that sometimes failure is the greatest masterpiece of all.

Booting Up History

For as long as Theodore Williams—Theo to family and friends—could remember, the Altair 8800 had been a monument in the basement's corner. It was dusty, mysterious, and utterly untouchable. His dad, a self-proclaimed computer pioneer, had warned everyone in the family never to mess with it.

"It holds everything," he'd said ominously.

Whether "everything" referred to the beginnings of the family tree or a hidden bank account in Switzerland, Theo wasn't sure. What he did know was that his dad's warning made the Altair irresistible.

At 19 years of age, Theo finally decided he'd had enough of the mystery.

After all, what was the point of family heirlooms if you couldn't exploit them for personal amusement? With a screwdriver in one hand and a cup of coffee in the other, he descended into the basement, prepared to finally crack the code.

Theo spent the first half-hour just figuring out how to turn the thing on. The Altair 8800 looked like it belonged in a museum, with its blinking lights and an array of switches that resembled a 1970s spaceship control panel. Finally, after consulting a Reddit forum titled "Altair 8800 for Dummies," he flipped the right combination of switches. The machine buzzed to life like Frankenstein's monster.

Theo plugged the Altair into a modern monitor using an adapter he wasn't entirely sure wouldn't cause an electrical fire. Miraculously, it worked.

Green text blinked on the screen, inviting him into the abyss with "ENTER PASSWORD."

Of course, there was a password.

Theo tried every obvious family connection: birthdays, anniversaries, the family dog's name. Nothing worked.

Then, as a joke, he typed "password."

The screen blinked for a moment.

"ACCESS GRANTED."

"Dad, you are an absolute dinosaur," Theo muttered. "Who even does that?"

A text-based menu that read greeted Theo:

Family History

Financial Records

Secrets

Games

Recipes

Naturally, Theo went straight for option three. It sounded far juicier than a dusty family history or a collection of casserole recipes. He hit "Enter," and a new menu appeared:

Dad's Secrets

Mom's Secrets

Grandma's Secrets

Miscellaneous Blackmail Material

"Grandma's Secrets" felt like the obvious choice. What could an 80-year-old matriarch possibly have hidden? It turned out quite a lot.

The file is labelled "GRANDMA_BLACKJACK.pdf" revealed a series of scanned Polaroids from the 1990s showing Theo's sweet, cookie-baking grandmother sitting at a blackjack table in the recently open casino, The Star, in

Sydney. She had a cigarette in one hand, a pile of chips in front of her, and an expression that said, "I own this place."

Excited by the find, Theo scrolled further to find a document titled "BLACKJACK_STRATEGY_GUIDE.DOC" with detailed instructions on how to count cards. Attached was a spreadsheet of her lifetime earnings: $243,000.

Theo leaned back in his chair, stunned. "Grandma was a high roller?"

Apparently, she'd used the winnings to pay for his dad's university tuition, which explained why his father got so defensive when anyone brought up their lunches at The Star.

Next, Theo clicked on Mom's Secrets. What he found was a series of encrypted files with names like "OPERATION_LEMON_DROP" and "SUBURBAN_ESPIONAGE."

One file had been partially decrypted, and the contents made Theo choke on his coffee. It was an extensive report detailing the neighbourhood's drama in the 1990s. There were detailed logs about Mrs Blunt stealing hydrangeas from Mr Giuseppe's garden, annotated maps of suspected extra-marital rendezvous, and even grainy photographs taken from the family's station wagon.

The best entry that Theo found almost floored him. It read: "April 14, 1998 – Mrs Dunphy's trash day. Recovered evidence of a secret shopping spree at David Jones. Also, why does she buy so much makeup?"

"I always thought Mum was just really into neighbourhood watch," Theo muttered. "Turns out she was running her own CIA."

Finally, Theo clicked on Dad's Secrets, hoping to uncover something as dramatic as Grandma's gambling or Mom's spy antics. Instead, he found an extensive archive of Dungeons & Dragons campaigns.

One folder, labelled "THE GREAT FAMILY BETRAYAL," seemed to look promising. As Theo read through it, he realised it wasn't a fictional campaign. It was a real-life game his dad had run with Theo and his siblings when they were kids.

The "betrayal" in question?

Apparently, his older sister Becky had cheated during a pivotal battle, and his dad had meticulously documented her crime as if to keep it for posterity.

The file ended with a simple note that was both scary and mostly quite intriguing and surely Dad. "One day, justice will prevail." That is all.

"I knew Becky didn't roll a natural 20," Theo said, shaking his fist. He made a mental note to confront her at the next family dinner.

By now, Theo was both entertained and slightly horrified. He clicked on Miscellaneous Blackmail Material with trepidation.

It turned out to be a collection of old family videos, heavily annotated with snarky commentary. One video showed Theo at age seven, attempting to perform magic tricks at a birthday party. The annotation read: "Theo's Magic Show Disaster, 1999. Watch at 3:42 for epic balloon animal fail."

This was followed by another one, which was a grainy clip of his uncle attempting to dance at a recent wedding, which Theo could not remember, captioned: "Why we don't let Uncle Jerry near an open bar."

After recovering from the initial information just obtained, Theo finally clicked on Recipes, expecting it to be the most boring section. Instead, he discovered a file titled "SECRET FAMILY RECIPE – DO NOT SHARE."

It was a recipe for the family's famous holiday cookies, but with an unexpected twist. The secret ingredient?

A splash of bourbon.

The file included a note from his dad: "Kids never noticed. Adults always thought the cookies were amazing. Coincidence? I think not."

Theo groaned. "We've been eating boozy cookies since kindergarten. That explains so much."

By the time Theo finished exploring the Altair 8800, he had learned more about his family than he ever thought possible. He decided to share the highlights at the next family gathering.

When Theo revealed his findings at the dinner table, he was met with a mix of laughter, outrage, and a fair amount of denial.

His dad refused to acknowledge the password debacle.

His mom defended her spy logs, said, "It was for the greater good."

Grandma just shrugged and said, "What happens in Vegas stays in Vegas. Unless you're smart enough to document it."

As for Theo?

He finally became the unofficial family historian and was promptly forbidden from touching any other heirlooms.

Survival

Two feline shadows moved silently through the underbrush. The first one, a sleek, silver-coated tabby, led the way, her luminous eyes scanning for danger.

Behind her padded a robust ginger cat whose every step betrayed his unease.

"Are you sure about this, Duchess Fluffington?" Sir Whiskersworth whispered; his voice was low but sharp.

"What choice do we have, Sir Whiskersworth? We have nothing," Duchess replied.

Sir Whiskersworth looked at the Duchess but said nothing and continue to follow her.

The two cats approached a solitary cottage, its garden bursting with vegetables. A plump hen clucked lazily in a coop nearby. Duchess Fluffington crouched low, ready to pounce, her tail twitching as she eyed the hen.

Sir Whiskersworth rushed and stopped in front of her.

"This feels wrong. They'll know it was us. What if they come after the colony? All will be for naught."

Duchess Fluffington hissed at him.

"Tonight is about survival, Sir Whiskersworth. If you're scared, and unwilling to do what it takes, well then, go back. I'll do it myself."

Sir Whiskersworth stepped back to let her pass and watched as Duchess Fluffington crept closer to the coop. Her movements were graceful, calculated. She reached for the latch and began working to open it.

Just as the coop door opened, Sir Whiskersworth bounded forward, blocking her path.

"Stop it! You are better than this, Duchess Fluffington."

Duchess Fluffington froze, her eyes narrowing. "What are you talking about? We need this. Think of the colony!"

"No. We need to think. If we steal from the humans, they'll hunt us. But if we trust them, they might help. I have seen the farmer leave scraps sometimes. Let's try asking for help instead of making enemies."

Duchess Fluffington wanted to find fault with his logic, but instead she sighed, her posture relaxing. "Fine. We'll do it your way. But if this doesn't work..."

"It will work. I am sure and if it doesn't, we'll find another way. Together."

Reluctantly, Duchess Fluffington followed Sir Whiskersworth back to the edge of the clearing. The two cats sat there, their silhouettes outlined by the rising sun, waiting for the farmer to emerge.

When the door creaked open and a kind-faced man stepped out, Sir Whiskersworth let out a soft, plaintive meow. The farmer paused, then smiled, tossing a handful of scraps toward them. Duchess Fluffington glanced at Sir Whiskersworth, her eyes softening.

"Maybe you're right," she murmured.

Magical Chaos

Last year's annual Christmas party at Colby & Co. was legendary, for all the wrong reasons, but it had a fantastic end.

The party started innocently enough.

The conference room was festively decorated with tinsel, blinking lights, and a suspiciously lopsided plastic tree that looked like it had lost a fight.

There was a Kris Kringle secret exchange with a $50 limit, which meant a lot of folks would be just spending $20.

Brenda from marketing brought her infamous fruitcake, which everyone hated, and was secretly used as a doorstop.

Then Ted, from accounting, spiked the fruit punch with jalapeño vodka, which embolden the CEO to challenge the new intern to a karaoke battle, fortunately stopped by the HR manager.

Things took a turn when someone suggested a holiday trivia game. Jerry, the IT guy, took it way too seriously and accused Linda from payroll of googling answers.

"You can't just know that reindeer have hollow fur!" he exclaimed, pointing an accusatory finger.

Linda threw a candy cane at him, and soon, an all-out peppermint war erupted.

Meanwhile, the karaoke machine was fired up. Steve from sales, encouraged by one too many cups of "safe" fruit punch, attempted George Michael's Last Christmas while dedicating the song to Emily, the mail sorter he has a crush on. The machine short-circuited mid-high note, leaving everyone's ears ringing and the fire alarm blaring. Luckily, the alarm was turned off before the fire department was called.

As if that weren't enough, someone—no one would admit who—let a huge golden retriever into the room. The dog made a beeline for the buffet, knocking over trays of mini meat pies and bacon-wrapped sausages. He then tangled himself in the tree lights, dragging the sad plastic tree across the room.

By 9 PM, the party was a disaster zone.

Steve was sulking in a corner because Emily had not even taken notice of his attempt to 'woo her'. To top it off, he had a sore throat from singing.

Jerry and Linda were locked in a heated debate over trivia rules, and the freaking dog was stuck under the copier, still trailing tinsel. It was shaping up to be the worst party in Colby & Co.'s history.

Then it happened.

A sudden gust of cold air swept through the room, extinguishing the blinking lights. Everyone froze. In the corner, the mangled plastic tree glowed softly. A tiny, glowing figure emerged.

A Christmas fairy, no taller than a stapler, her wings shimmering with stardust.

"Colby & Co., your holiday spirit is in shambles," she squeaked, her voice like the tinkling of sleigh bells.

With a flick of her wand, the room transformed. The broken karaoke machine burst to life, playing festive classics in perfect harmony. The buffet refilled itself, complete with a mountain of chocolate truffles. The dog reappeared, tinsel-free and wagging his tail happily.

The fairy flitted over to Jerry and Linda. "Make peace!" she demanded. They reluctantly shook hands, and Jerry even laughed at one of Linda's corny jokes.

By the end of the night, the office was buzzing with cheer. People sang, laughed, and shared stories about their chaotic year. As the clock struck midnight, the fairy disappeared in a puff of glitter, leaving behind a single note:

"Remember: even chaos can be magical with the right spirit."

Spaced Out

Emma's face pressed against something cold and metallic. She rolled over and stared up at a strange ceiling covered in softly blinking lights. She sat up quickly and called out, "Max."

From across the room, Max responded, "Emma, if this is a prank, it's not funny."

Emma got up and walked over to Max, who seemed to be sprawled on what looked like a floating cot. His hair was sticking out in ten different directions, and his pyjamas—a pair of sweatpants and a faded "World's Best Boyfriend" t-shirt.

"Come on, Max, wake up. Something's wrong," Emma said, shaking him to no avail.

"I don't want to go to work," Max mumbled with his eyes closed.

"Max!" Emma yelled, and he finally sat up.

"What... What's happening? Did we go to a weird Airbnb or something? I remember nothing. Do you, Em?"

"No," was her response.

Max looked around, his eyes widening as he took in the room. The walls were smooth and curved and had a few monitors displaying indecipherable symbols.

Emma walks over to a window. A sprawling view of endless stars, a distant planet spinning lazily in the void, greets well at least what looked like a window.

"Max," she said, "We're in space."

Max stared for a long moment. Then he burst out laughing.

"Good one, Em. Did you sign us up for one of those escape room things? Is there a guy in a costume who's going to jump out and yell 'ALIENS!'?"

Emma walked up to Max, grabbed him by his arm, and pushed him to the window. "Does this look like an escape room to you? Does it, Max?"

"Oh... Oh no. Nope. Nope, nope, nope. I don't do space. I get motion sickness in elevators!"

Before Emma could reply, a cheerful, robotic voice echoed through the room.

"Good morning, occupants! Welcome aboard Space Station Zorblatt-9. You are currently orbiting the beautiful planet Snerklorp. We hope you had a pleas-ant journey."

"Did... did that wall just talk?" Max whispered.

The voice continued. "Your mission, should you choose to accept it, is to—Oh, who are we kidding? You already accepted! Just so you know, your memories of the past 48 hours were erased for security reasons. You're welcome!"

"Excuse me!" Emma shouted. "What do you mean, we accepted? And what mission?"

"Great questions. Unfortunately, I'm just the automated greeting program. For further assistance, please proceed to the Command Deck."

A door slid open.

Max stared at it, then at Emma. "I don't trust it. It's like when cats knock things over on purpose. They know something you don't."

"Do you have a better idea, Max? Because I'd love to hear it."

Max opened his mouth. "No, I do not, but if we die, I'm haunting you."

Emma and Max walked through the door into a hallway that seemed endless. They passed doors marked in alien script, but they did not open any of them and kept walking down the hallway until they reached a large room filled with blinking monitors, strange instruments, and... a vending machine?

"Finally! Snacks!" Max rushed over and saw the machine had only one button labelled "FLARP" punched it, and was rewarded with a shiny, neon-green bar.

"That looks toxic," Emma said, wrinkling her nose.

"I'm starving, and it's free," said Max as he took a bite.

He quickly spat it out: "Nope! Bad idea. Tastes like feet. Alien feet."

Before Emma could comment, a hologram flickered to life in the centre of the room. It was a creature that looked like a cross between an otter and a librarian, complete with glasses perched on what might have been its face.

"Greetings, Earthlings! I am Commander Bilsthorpe. You have been chosen for a most noble mission."

Emma looked at the strange being and said, "Oh yeah, about that, mister. Max and I do not remember agreeing to any mission, and we don't even know how we got here!"

Bilsthorpe adjusted its glasses and smiled—well, what looked like a smile since the creature only had two teeth. "Ah, yes. That is a common reaction among your species. Rest assured, the Galactic Council chose you for your exceptional qualities."

"Exceptional? Us? You got to be kidding. No, we are plain and common, not exceptional. Why, just last week, I locked myself out of our apartment," remarked Max.

"And I cannot even boil water to make spaghetti!" Emma added.

"Be that as it may, you were selected because of your compatibility as a team," answered the commander.

"A team?" Max muttered. "We can't even agree on what to watch on Netflix."

"Your mission is to deliver this package to the planet Snerklorp. It contains vital information that will prevent an intergalactic catastrophe."

Suddenly, a drawer opened, revealing a small, glowing cube. Emma was reaching for it when the commander shouted: "Careful! That cube is highly sensitive. Do not shake it, drop it, or expose it to music with excessive bass."

Max frowned. "What happens if we do?"

Commander Bilsthorpe's hologram otter hands showed an expanding motion and simply said: "Boom."

Emma grabbed the cube carefully. "Okay, so how do we get to this so called Snerklorp?"

Bilsthorpe gestured toward a sleek, egg-shaped pod. "That transport will take you there. Good luck, Earthlings. The fate of the galaxy depends on you!"

The hologram disappeared.

"Great," Max said. "If we are the galaxy's last hope, we're doomed."

The pod ride was uneventful, except for Max's constant complaints about the lack of seat cushions. They landed on Snerklorp with a soft thud, greeted by a crowd of aliens who cheered as they emerged.

"Wow," Max said, "They really rolled out the red carpet for us."

One alien stepped forward, holding what looked like a clipboard. "Did you bring the package?"

Emma handed over the cube, and the alien examined it, then nodded. "Thank you for your service. You may now return to Earth."

"Wait a minute. That's it? We don't get a medal, or a parade or something?"

The alien looked at Max and pointed to another door marked "Gift Shop." "You may take one complimentary souvenir from the gift shop."

The gift shop was a tiny room filled with questionable items. Emma chose a mug that had imprinted on it I Saved the Galaxy and All I Got Was This Mug, while Max chose a stuffed alien that looked like a potato.

As they boarded the pod to return home, Max sighed. "Well, that was... weird."

Emma smirked. "Weird? Max, we just saved the galaxy. I think we've peaked."

Back on Earth and a day later, they woke up in their own bed; the events of the past day feeling like a strange dream. Except for the mug and the stuffed potato alien sitting on their nightstand.

Max picked up the potato alien and grinned. "Did it really happen, Emma?"

Emma groaned, reach for the nightstand drawer and took out some weed. She stared at it for a moment. "Max, promise me if we ever smoke this stuff again, let's make sure someone else is in the room."

"Deal," Max said, "But next time we space out, I'm bringing snacks from home."

Shock Therapy

Frank watched the rise and fall of Elizabeth's chest. The soft rhythm of her breath was a stark contrast to the storm raging within him. She lay there, pale and still. The doctor stood beside him; his face etched with concern.

"She's stable for now, Mr Evans," the doctor said, his voice a gentle murmur. "But we need to monitor her closely. She suffered a significant head injury."

Frank nodded. He had never felt so helpless. His Lizzie had not opened her eyes in weeks.

Suddenly, a soft voice broke the silence. "Je suis si fatiguée," a voice whispered, the words unfamiliar yet strangely familiar.

Frank's heart leaped. "Elizabeth?" he asked, his voice barely a whisper as his eyes darted to her face.

She stirred, her eyelids fluttering open. Her gaze, once so warm and inviting, now held a vacant, almost otherworldly quality. Then she spoke again, this time in a thick, foreign accent. "Oui, mon cher. C'est moi."

Frank's jaw dropped. Elizabeth, his wife—the epitome of Australian twang and laid-back slang—was now speaking fluent French.

"Elizabeth," he stammered, "what on earth are you talking about?"

The doctor, who had been observing the exchange with growing interest, stepped forward. "Mr. Evans, it's possible that Elizabeth has developed Foreign Accent Syndrome as a result of her head injury."

Frank's confusion deepened. "Foreign Accent Syndrome? What's that?"

"It's a rare neurological condition where a person's speech pattern changes, often taking on a foreign accent. It's caused by damage to the brain's language centres. We must run some tests."

The doctor left the room to prepare for a series of tests. Left alone with Elizabeth, Frank attempted to strike up a conversation.

"So, uh, comment ça va?" he asked, his French pronunciation a comical blend of Aussie slang and Parisian chic.

Elizabeth raised an eyebrow. "Vous parlez français?" she asked, her accent growing stronger.

"Well, not really," Frank admitted. "But I'm trying to learn. I thought, you know, we could practice together."

Elizabeth chuckled. "Très bien. Alors, dis-moi, qu'est-ce que tu as fait hier soir?"

Frank's face turned a deep shade of red. "Um, I, uh, watched the footy. And ate a meat pie. And drank a few beers."

Elizabeth's eyes widened. "Du football Australien et une tourte à la viande? C'est très exotique!"

Frank nodded, feeling increasingly out of his depth. "Yeah, it's pretty exotic, I guess. So, what about you? What do you want to talk about today?"

Elizabeth paused, a thoughtful expression on her face. "Hier, j'ai visité le Louvre. Puis, j'ai dîné au Tour d'Argent."

Frank's jaw dropped. "The Louvre? And the Tour d'Argent? You want to go to Paris?"

Elizabeth shrugged. "Oui, pourquoi pas?"

The doctor walked back in to speak to Frank.

"Mr Evans, I just checked, and your medical insurance does not fully cover the fees associated with the tests I need to run, so I thought I'd check with you first to make sure I can proceed with the treatment."

"Well, Doctor, how much does my medical insurance do not cover?"

The doctor looked at Emily and then at Frank and softly gave him the amount: "$132,435.17."

Frank was taken aback, but before he could answer, Elizabeth answered for him. "Oi, doc! You're off your rocker if you think I'm gonna let you charge me husband a bloody fortune to fix me head!"

Frank's eyes widened. "Elizabeth! You are cured!" he exclaimed.

"Cured? What do you mean, 'cured' Frank? Why am I in the hospital?"

With the help of the doctor, Frank explained what happened, how she spoke French and how miraculously she now was OK.

Emily looked at the doctor and asked: "Oi doc, then I can go home?"

The doctor nodded and left both Frank and Elizabeth smiling and embracing each other.

As the doctor turned around the corner, he smiled and muttered to himself, "Nothing like shock therapy to cure a person."

The Key

The sun dappled through the curtains, casting playful shadows on the freshly painted walls. Emily and Alex, young and hopeful, stood in the heart of their new home, a quaint cottage nestled in a quiet suburban street. The scent of fresh paint mingled with the earthy aroma of the old hardwood floors, promising a fresh start.

As they explored their new domain, excitement bubbled within them. They had brought a few boxes with them they wanted to be sure would not get lost during the move.

Alex's dad had said: "Be sure you do your own moving of the important stuff. Can't trust the movers. They lose things."

Alex had told Emily what his father had said, and she'd agreed. So here they were, bringing 12 boxes and a few clothes and towels into their new home. The boxes contained pictures, albums, and memories of their youth. Of course, they'd also brought some practical stuff, like cans of food and one pot and skillet, so they could make some lunch, and the old, trusted microwave to make popcorn. The latter was Alex's idea, for he knew Emily was a popcorn lover.

As they wandered around each room, they felt the promise of a new chapter in each room, a blank canvas waiting to be filled with their love and laughter.

Emily told Alex how she wanted each room laid out and wondered if she could have the smallest bedroom for a study.

"Why do you need a study, Emily? You never said you wanted one?"

"I don't know Alex. I... I just feel like I should have one. I am not sure why, but I just do."

"Darling, if that is what you want, then that is what you will have. I will even make popcorn and bring it to you in your new domain. How's that?"

"You are wonderful," she said with a smile and gave him a big kiss.

"Now let's hang up these few clothes we brought."

It was in the bedroom closet, while hanging up the few articles they had brought with them, that they stumbled upon a surprise.

Taped to the wall, a small, antique key glinted in the dim light. Attached to it was a faded piece of paper with a single, intriguing sentence: "Find the treasure."

A shiver of excitement ran through them. A treasure hunt in their own home? Who'd left the key? The key had ignited their curiosity.

"I am going to call the real estate agent maybe she knows what this is about?" exclaimed Alex, taking out his mobile phone, but Emily placed her hand on his phone.

"Wait, sweetie. This might be fun," she remarked. "Why spoilt it? She might just want to drive here and see for herself. Where is your sense of adventure? Besides, we have time. The movers are not coming till tomorrow. Let's see what we find."

Alex could not refuse his bride of seven years. She was always the adventurous one, the dreamer, so the search began in earnest. They combed through every nook and cranny, from the master bedroom to the garage and all the rooms. They examined every kitchen drawer, every kitchen cupboard, every hidden corner. The house, once familiar, now seemed to hold secrets, inviting them to uncover its hidden depths.

After hours of searching, their hopes dwindled. The treasure, it seemed, was elusive. Disappointed but not defeated, they took a break. As they sat on the floor, sipping a soft drink and eating some popcorn, Emily's eyes fell upon the open pantry door. There she saw it. A small hole, barely visible.

"I think I found something," she said, getting up.

She rushed to the pantry, reached into the small recess, and pulled out a small, worn envelope. Inside, they found a handwritten note, its ink faded with age. The letter spoke of a writer, a dreamer, who had once called this house their own. He had poured their heart and soul into their stories, crafting worlds of magic and wonder and he left them this note, hoping they would continue in his journey, for the note contained a list of story ideas for the new owners to write their own stories.

It was simply signed: "José."

Alex looked at Emily. "Wow, how about that? I was hoping for gold bullion, not a note with a couple of dozens of writing prompts," he said, disappointed.

Emily, however, felt different. A surge of inspiration coursed through Emily as they read the note and the prompts for stories.

We aren't just moving into a new house, we're inheriting a literary legacy, she thought.

"Alex, I am going to do just what this note says." Clutching the key in her hand, she said, "Come on. We are going to buy a new desktop."

"A new desktop? Why?" queried Alex.

"Because I feel the urge to write," was all Emily said as they walked out the door and locked up.

The next day, the movers came and unloaded all the furniture and boxes, with Emily directing them what piece of furniture went where, like a police officer directing traffic.

Alex's dad was there with a clipboard, checking off articles as they were unloading, not trusting the movers to do their job.

Emily was in one of the converted rooms setting up her new desktop in her new study and, as she did, she felt she was making a connection to the previous owner/writer who had come before them. She thought she could almost hear his thoughts, his ideas, his dreams, and his aspirations. The note, with its story prompts, was a gift, a challenge, and an opportunity for both Emily and Alex.

After a few weeks, they settled in and, inspired by the writer's passion, Emily authored her own stories, weaving her own tales into the fabric of the house's history.

She typed away on her desktop and munched on her popcorn that Alex had brought.

The cottage, once a mere dwelling, became a sanctuary for her creativity. The key they found had led them not to gold or jewels, but to a far more precious gift: the gift of storytelling.

Thanks, José, Emily thought as she pounded her keyboard, wherever you are.

Personal Ad

Desperate Stepdad Seeks Suitable Suitors (Prefer-ably with Excellent Medical)

Listen, folks, I'm a man on a mission. I'm trying to launch my two lovely stepdaughters into the world of wedded bliss. They're splendid girls, really. I swear.

Exhibit A (45, going on fabulous): Smart as a whip, successful career (I won't bore you with the details, but it involves management skills galore and power suits, so you know she's got her life together). Comes with one (adorable, mostly) pre-teen bonus package (9 years old, loves video games and questioning every-thing—sounds familiar, right?). Seeking a man who isn't afraid of a little... seasoning. Must be comfortable with the phrase "early bedtime," both his own and hers. Bonus points if you know how to unclog a drain.

Exhibit B (43, and holding strong): Equally smart, equally successful (unique skills set, different power suits, but the same impressive bank account). Adores her niece (the aforementioned bonus package). Seeking a man who appreciates an excellent wine, a terrible pun, and the occasional spontaneous road trip. Must be able to tolerate her sister (see Exhibit A) and me (I'm harmless, I promise... mostly). Double bonus points if you own a Mini. Or a cabin in the woods. Or, hell, even a decent grill.

What they both offer: Enjoyable conversation, excel-lent cooking skills (they do order takeout often though), and the unwavering love of a slightly over-bearing but well-meaning stepfather (that's me!).

What I offer: My eternal gratitude, a heartfelt toast at the wedding (I've been practicing), and the promise to stay out of their business (mostly).

What I DON'T offer: Any refunds. This is a final sale.

Serious inquiries only (although a good sense of humour is necessary).

Please send photos of your face showing your teeth (just kidding... mostly). Respond with your CV and bank account details, and your favourite stepdad joke. If you can make me laugh, you've got a shot.

P.S. If you're independently wealthy and own an exclusive island, please skip the CV and just send the co-ordinates.

All enquiries should be submitted to:

springfarm14@gmail.com

Flirt

Cecil waggled his prolegs suggestively at Clementine. "Say, Clementine, you got any plans after we... you know... pupate?"

Clementine twitched a mandible. "I plan to eat this particularly delectable leaf. It's a fine vintage, you see." She delicately nibbled the edge.

Cecil sidled closer, bumping her slightly. "Oh, I see. A female of refined tastes. I appreciate that. I, myself, am quite the connoisseur of... well, leaves, of course. But also... other things." He winked, or at least did what a caterpillar considered winking, which involved slightly twitching an antenna.

Clementine sighed, a sound like a tiny leaf rustling. "Look, Cecil, I'm trying to focus here. This leaf isn't going to eat itself."

"But imagine," Cecil persisted, inching closer still, "imagine us, after our... transformation. Fluttering amongst the flowers, sipping nectar, even... dancing in the breeze." He attempted a little wiggle, which mostly just made him wobble precariously on the branch.

Clementine's eye stalks drooped. "Dancing? Cecil, you're practically glued to this branch. You're not exactly Baryshnikov."

"Ah, but that's now!" Cecil exclaimed. "Imagine me with wings! I'll be a veritable aerial acrobat! I'll... I'll write your name in the sky with my flight patterns!"

Clementine shuddered. "That sounds... sticky."

Cecil, undeterred, pressed on. "And the colours! Imagine our wings! Mine will be a vibrant emerald green, complementing your... well, whatever colour your wings will be. I'm sure they'll be... adequate."

Clementine's skin felt tight. A strange tingling sensation ran through her tiny caterpillar body. "Cecil," she said slowly, "I think I'm... changing."

"Oh, excellent!" Cecil rubbed his front prolegs together. "We can emerge together! Like... like two peas in a... well, you know."

But Clementine wasn't listening. The tingling intensified. Her skin hardened, forming a chrysalis. "Finally," she muttered from within the hardening shell, "some peace and quiet."

Cecil, oblivious, continued his monologue. "I've always envisioned our first flight together. We'll soar above the meadow, hand... or rather, wing in wing. We'll..."

He stopped, noticing the now fully formed chrysalis. "Clementine? You in there? Should I practice my aerial calligraphy?"

A few days later, a beautiful monarch butterfly emerged from the chrysalis. Clementine stretched her vibrant orange and black wings, took one look at the branch where Cecil was still very much a caterpillar, and with a flick of her wings, soared into the sky.

Cecil watched her go. A single tear, or rather, a single drop of caterpillar goo, rolling down his face.

"I guess she wasn't a fan of my flirt," he mumbled.

The Gazebo

The Northport Gazette, 1925, blared the headline: "PROMINENT CITIZEN PAUL MORTLOCK PERISHED IN PARK!"

Paul, a man whose prominence was mostly self proclaimed and based on his ownership of the town's only haberdashery, had met an untimely end beneath a grumpy gum tree in the local park. The circumstances were... unclear.

Some town folk whispered of a rogue cricket ball, others of a disgruntled cravat customer. Officially, it was ruled "death by misadventure," a catch-all phrase that covered everything from spontaneous combustion to tripping over one's own top hat.

To commemorate Paul (and perhaps to distract from the park's newfound reputation for lethal mishaps), the Northport Council, in their infinite wisdom, erected a gazebo.

"The Paul Memorial Gazebo," a brass plaque declared. It was a fine structure, all wrought iron, and swirling flourishes, perfect for romantic trysts and avoiding sudden downpours.

Except for one slight problem: Paul.

Paul, despite his earthly demise, wasn't quite ready to leave Northport Park. He'd taken up residence in his gazebo. Not in a spooky, chain-rattling way, mind you. Paul was more of a spectral nuisance.

He'd clear his throat loudly just as a couple were about to share their first kiss.

He'd materialize a ghostly trilby hat on a young man's head, causing his sweetheart to shriek.

He'd even occasionally rearrange the decorative ironwork into suggestive shapes, much to the horror of elderly ladies enjoying their afternoon conversations.

Generations of Northport lovers grew up with tales of "Paul's Gazebo." It was a place to be avoided after dusk, a source of local legends, and a constant headache for the council, who received a steady stream of complaints about "unexplained breezes" and "phantom haberdashery."

Fast forward to 2025: Northport Park was still there, the gazebo still stood (albeit with a few more coats of paint), and the legend of Paul persisted.

One early evening, a woman named Betty was walking through the park when she was tragically mugged and killed. Betty, like Paul before her, found herself tethered to the park, her spirit unable to move on.

Betty, however, was a vastly different ghost than Paul.

While he was a fussy, slightly pompous spirit, Betty was a no-nonsense, modern woman. She quickly realised Paul's presence.

"Honestly, clearing your throat? Is that the best you can do?" came Betty's voice.

Paul jumped. "Good heavens! Who... what...?"

"I'm Betty," she said. "And this," she gestured around the gazebo, "what you are doing is simply just ridiculous."

Paul replied, "I'll have you know this is a memorial! A tribute to a prominent..."

"A prominent haberdasher? Look, I get it. You're stuck. I'm stuck. But scaring teenagers and old ladies will solve nothing. Don't you agree?"

Over the next few weeks, an unlikely friendship blossomed between the two ghosts. Betty, with her modern sensibilities, helped Paul understand how his antics were perceived.

"You're not haunting," she explained, "you're just being a pest."

Paul told Betty about Northport's history, about the park's past, and about his own rather mundane life. He confessed that he wasn't prominent at all, simply a man who loved his shop and his town. He admitted he was scared and that he didn't know how to move on.

One evening, as the setting sun cast long shadows across the park, Betty had an idea.

"Paul," she said, "we're both stuck here because we have unfinished business, right?"

"I suppose so," Paul replied. "But what business could I possibly have after all this time?"

"Closure," Betty said. "We need closure."

She proposed they work together to find peace.

Betty, having been a social media manager in her living life, suggested they use their combined spectral energy to project a message into the digital world. They focused their combined energy and sent a message to the Northport Historical Society, who were intrigued by the message and investigated the gazebo.

The historical society, after some research, uncovered the true story of Paul's death. It wasn't a cricket ball, or a disgruntled customer. It was a loose branch from the grumpy gum tree dislodged by a strong gust of wind. A simple accident.

The revelation brought Paul a sense of peace he hadn't felt in a century. He finally understood that his death wasn't some grand conspiracy or a cosmic joke. It was just... an accident.

For Betty, helping Paul allowed her to come to terms with her own sudden and violent death. She found solace in helping another spirit find peace and in connecting with the living world again.

This new clarification on Paul's death gave the town of Northport a fresh a new purpose. They placed a new and larger plaque, but this time it commemorated the town's resilience and did not mention Paul as a prominent citizen.

The council made a big deal of the news that had finally 'solved' the death of Paul Mortlock, but this time, the new plaque gave a history of the town.

When dusk fell on the evening of the ceremony, Paul, and Betty sensed a profound unburdening.

At last, they were free to cross over together into the eternal light.

Bartholomew "Barty" Butterfield III sat at the table nursing his gin and tonic, while across from him sat Penelope "Penny" Plumtree-Smythe with her half-empty glass of Merlot. They were both writers, a fact they usually kept buried unless provoked during a polite small talk. Tonight, they sat there, venting.

"Another month without a single, solitary review," Barty sighed.

Penny nodded. "Tell me about it. I checked Goodreads too. Nothing. Not even a 'meh'."

They were both self-published authors.

Barty had penned what he considered his masterpiece, a historical romance titled "Lord Reginald's Enthusiastic Pickle," a book he was convinced was going to be a complete success.

Penny had written "The Curious Case of the Cryptic Crumpet," a cozy mystery that featured a whiskey, a tea-loving spinster and a series of suspiciously soggy pastries.

Both books were available on Amazon and, according to their mothers, had covers that were "quite fetching," and while they had a few sales, both books were languishing in the digital abyss of no reviews.

"It's like we're shouting into a void," Barty lamented.

"Merely existing, I'm starting to think my crumpet is cursed," Penny added.

Had their marketing been insufficient? Had they chosen the wrong font for their titles? Were people simply not interested in enthusiastic pickles or cryptic crumpets?

"Perhaps we're simply ahead of our time. Like Van Gogh. Unappreciated in our own era, destined for posthumous fame," lamented Barty.

"Except Van Gogh sold at least one painting to his brother," Penny pointed out. She sighed. "You know what, Barty?"

"What?" answered Barty as he downed the last of his drink.

"I haven't even sold one eBook this month. Unless you count my mother's accidental double purchase."

"Barkeep," said Barty, motioning. "Two more."

When the drinks arrived, they began brainstorming increasingly absurd marketing strategies.

"We could hire a skywriter," Barty suggested, his eyes gleaming with a manic intensity. "Imagine: 'Read Lord Reginald's Enthusiastic Pickle!' written across the sky!"

"And what about mine?" Penny retorted. "'Solve the Mystery of the Cryptic Crumpet!' emblazoned on a giant inflatable crumpet floating over Sydney Harbour?"

The conversation spiralled into a vortex of more ridiculous ideas that included guerrilla marketing campaigns involving strategically placed pickle jars, flash mobs dressed as crumpets, and even a joint venture where they would deliver signed copies of their books to unsuspecting strangers.

Suddenly, a lone figure approached their table. He was a small, wiry man with a pair of thick glasses perched on his nose and a perpetually bewildered expression.

"Excuse me," he said, his voice barely above a whisper. "Are you... the pickle and crumpet people?"

Barty and Penny exchanged a look of stunned disbelief. Had their outlandish brainstorming somehow manifested this strange encounter?

"We are authors," Barty corrected, puffing out his chest slightly. "I wrote 'Lord Reginald's Enthusiastic Pickle,' and this is Penelope Plumtree-Smythe, author of 'The Curious Case of the Cryptic Crumpet.'"

The man's eyes widened behind his glasses. "Oh, my goodness! I've been looking for you everywhere!" He pulled two well-worn paperbacks from his satchel. "I'm a member of the local book club, and we just finished reading both of your books!"

Barty and Penny were speechless. Finally, after months of agonizing silence, someone had read their work!

"We loved them!" the man continued; his voice filled with genuine enthusiasm. "The pickle was... surprisingly poignant, and the crumpet mystery kept us guessing until the very end!"

Barty felt a lump forming in his throat. Penny's eyes were glistening with unshed tears. This was it. This was the validation they had been craving.

"We were going to write reviews," the man explained, "but... well..." He shuffled his feet nervously. "We accidentally set them on fire."

"Set them on fire?" Barty repeated, his voice a strangled whisper.

"Yes," the man confirmed, nodding vigorously. "We were having a book club meeting by the fireplace, and... well, Mrs. Higgins tripped, and... long story short, your books are now providing warmth for her cat."

Barty and Penny stared at each other; the initial euphoria was replaced by a profound sense of bewilderment. They had finally found their readers, only to discover that their reviews literally went up in smoke.

"Well, it has been a pleasure. Bye for now," said the man as he walked away.

Barty and Penny could only nod mutely.

"Barkeep," said Barty, motioning. "Two more."

"How about that," said Penny.

"Yeah, how about that? We at least know our books had provided some warmth, even if it was for a cat."

Perfect Job

It was a crisp autumn night, and count Vladimir von Dracula, a vampire of the most ancient and aristocratic lineage, soared gracefully through the moonlit Northport NSW sky. He was gliding over a dark forest, his long cape trailing behind him like an ominous shadow. His mind wandered to an existential question: Was he overdoing it with the cape?

Distracted, Vladimir didn't notice the sturdy oak tree in his flight path until it was too late. With a resounding whack, he collided headfirst into an outstretched branch, spinning out of control like an uncoordinated bat. He plummeted to the forest floor in an unceremonious heap, his cape wrapping around him like a defective parachute.

When he woke up, the world seemed... different. Fuzzy. The darkness of the forest was less comforting and more... murky. The stars weren't twinkling with their usual malice; they were just, well, twinkling. And his teeth felt strangely dull. Rubbing his throbbing head, he groggily stumbled to his feet. He felt lightheaded and parched.

"What happened?" he muttered, his voice lacking the usual guttural authority. He felt... mortal. And extremely thirsty.

He stumbled out of the forest and walked into the small town of Northport, NSW. As he wandered the streets, he came upon a glass window with a bright red sign: HELP WANTED: Blood Bank Technician – No Experience Necessary!

"Blood?" he whispered, his parched throat practically singing the word. It sounded perfect, though he did not know why.

As a matter of fact, what is my name? He wondered. With nothing but instinct driving him, he pushed open the door.

Inside, a bored receptionist looked up from her magazine. "Can I help you?"

"I am... here for the blood," he said, his eyes gleaming.

She raised an eyebrow. "You mean the job?"

"Yes. The job. That is... exactly what I mean."

She handed him a clipboard. "Fill this out."

He stared at the paper and froze at the first question: first name, initial, and surname. What was his name? Quickly, he made up a name: Mildred M. Mortis and completed the form and gave it back to the receptionist, who looked at it, gave him a look, and started the interview process.

"OK. Let's confirm some of these questions. First your name again."

"Mildred M. Mortis."

She narrowed her eyes. "Are you lying?"

"No," Mildred said, looking as sincere as a man in a tattered cape could.

"What does the 'M' stand for, anyway?"

Without hesitation Mildred answered, "Moonbeam."

"Moonbeam," repeated the nurse.

"Yes. That is correct. Mildred Moonbeam Mortis is my name."

"Okay, Mr. Mortis. Do you have any relevant experience?"

"Oh, yes," Mildred said confidently. "I have handled blood for a very long time."

"Have you worked in a medical setting before?"

"No, but I have collected blood. Personally."

She gave him a sceptical look but wrote something down. "Any allergies?"

"Garlic," he said without thinking.

"Okay, Mildred. Now, why do you want to work here?"

Mildred hesitated. He couldn't very well said, "Because I'm desperately thirsty and inexplicably drawn to blood." So, he improvised. "I wish to... help humanity. Yes, help humanity with its blood... needs."

The receptionist seemed unimpressed, but handed him a visitor's badge. "Go talk to Dr. Henderson in the back. If he likes you, the job's yours."

Mildred wandered down the hallway until he found a small office marked "Dr Henderson." He knocked, and a man in a white coat looked up from his desk.

"Ah, you must be the applicant," Dr Henderson said, gesturing for him to sit. "Why don't you tell me about yourself?"

"I am Mildred M. Mortis, and I have a deep passion for... blood."

Dr Henderson raised an eyebrow. "Interesting. Do you have any medical training?"

"No, but I am very good with needles," Mildred said, suddenly remembering the time he once skewered an enemy through the heart with a silver-tipped spear.

"We can train you," Dr. Henderson said slowly. "But this job requires a lot of responsibility. People's lives depend on it."

"I understand," Mildred said solemnly. "I take blood seriously."

Something in his tone seemed to convince Dr Henderson, who stood and extended his hand. "Alright, Mildred. Welcome to the team."

Mildred stared at the outstretched hand for a moment, unsure what to do. Finally, he grasped it and gave an overly enthusiastic shake, nearly dislocating the doctor's shoulder.

On his first day, Mildred was given a tour of the facility. The blood bank was a bustling hive of activity, with technicians scurrying about, cataloguing donations, and preparing shipments. Mildred was put in charge of organizing the inventory.

It was paradise. The perfect job.

Rows upon rows of blood bags, neatly labelled and sorted by type, stretched before him. His thirst gnawed at him, but he resisted the urge to grab one and chug it like a juice box.

"Remember," Dr Henderson had said during orientation, "this blood is for patients in need. Not for personal use."

"Of course," Mildred had replied, though inside he felt like crying and did not know why.

As the days passed, Mildred settled into his new life and while he discovered the joys of coffee (a strange brew but oddly invigorating) he could not stop thinking of blood, so he developed a plan: He would replace the type Rhnull blood bags with tomato juice. And he would place a tiny little 'x' on the bottom of the label so he would not distribute it on any orders.

This idea worked beautifully for Mildred, and when you added the fact that he became popular with his coworkers, who found his old-fashioned manners charming, he was completely happy at his job.

One afternoon, as Mildred was alphabetising the AB-negative shelf, another technician burst into the room.

"We've got an emergency!" she cried. "The hospital is out of O-positive, and they need more now!"

Mildred sprang into action, gathering the required blood bags and loading them onto a cart and wheeled them to the delivery bay and he even helped load them onto the van, which drove off.

As he returned to his desk, he sighed.

He missed the thrill of the hunt and the dramatic flair of his vampire days, but he had everything he needed here, or so he thought.

Mildred felt suddenly thirsty and decided he needed a break and as he walked back to the blood shelves and was about to enter, Dr Henderson opened his office door and called out, "Mildred. In my office now!"

He walked into the office and sat in the chair Dr Henderson pointed to.

"Mildred," Dr Henderson said. "We've been monitoring the security footage. Care to explain why you've been replacing all the type Rhnull blood bags with tomato juice?"

"I... uh..." Mildred stammered, sweat beading on his pale forehead.

"And why you've been teaching the platelets to do synchronised swimming?"

"They showed real potential!" Mildred protested. "You should see their routine to 'Dancing Queen'!"

Dr Henderson sighed, sliding a paper across her desk. "And perhaps most concerning... why have you been organizing speed dating events between the A positive and O negative bags?"

"Love knows no blood type!" Mildred declared passionately. "Besides, their children would be universal donors!"

"You're fired," Dr Henderson said flatly. "And please stop putting wedding invitations on the plasma freezer."

As Mildred slouched toward the exit, he yelled at the doctor: "Fine. I'll take my talents to the mosquito farm instead. At least they appreciate a good blood sommelier," and then he muttered to himself. "I will miss the donuts."

As he closed the door behind him, he wondered: Is it normal to crave blood-flavoured donuts? And do they make them?

Murder Or Divorce

Miriam, Cathy, and Maria sat around the kitchen table, their monthly "Cuppa and Whine" afternoon well underway. The coffee was flowing, the biscuits almost gone, and the conversation had taken its usual turn toward the absurdities of life, love, and the peculiarities of their respective husbands.

"Honestly, sometimes I don't know if I'm married to a man or a child," Maria said, rolling her eyes. "I mean, yesterday he asked me if the dishwasher could wash his keyboard. His keyboard! Who does that?"

Cathy nearly choked on her biscuit and laughed. "At least he asked! Last week, mine saw the dishwasher was full and placed several pots in it with some clothes, and now the clothes smell of spaghetti."

Miriam had been unusually quiet, holding her mug, and staring out the patio door. Then she said, "You know, sometimes I think about divorce."

Cathy and Maria froze, mid-giggle, their expressions instantly sobering. Cathy reached out to touch Miriam's arm. "Oh, Miriam, are you okay? Is it that bad?"

Miriam took a long sip of her coffee and smirked. "Or murder."

The room fell silent for a moment before Maria burst into laughter so loud it drowned out the radio playing oldies on vintage FM 88.7.

"Murder? Miriam, you couldn't hurt a fly if it landed on you."

Miriam shrugged. "Flies don't leave their dirty underwear on the bathroom sink after I've asked them not to for the thousandth time."

Cathy leaned back in her chair, arms crossed, a sceptical grin on her face. "Okay, spill it. What's he done now?"

"Oh, where do I start?" Miriam sighed. "He forgot our anniversary last month, but he remembered the release date for that new Reacher season on Netflix. He reorganised the spice rack alphabetically because 'it makes more sense,' but he can't find the hamper. And—oh! Here's the kicker—last week, he tried to finish the work I was doing in the laundry and ended up flooding the room. Then he just stood there and said, 'Well, at least the floor is clean now.'"

Maria was laughing so hard she clutched her sides. "That sounds exactly like something my Marco would say! Last month, he 'fixed' the toaster by taking it apart, and now it's a paperweight. An extremely expensive paperweight."

Cathy snorted. "Oh, please. My Steve thinks he's a handyman, too. Last year, he installed a ceiling fan, but he didn't secure it properly. It flew off and nearly decapitated my mother who was visiting."

"Why are they all like this?" Miriam groaned, throwing her hands in the air. "Is it some secret husband initiation ceremony? 'Congratulations on your wedding. Here's your manual on how to drive your wife insane.'"

Cathy and Maria dissolved into laughter again, but as the giggles subsided, Maria looked at Miriam with a soft smile. "So, seriously. Divorce or murder—which is it going to be?"

Miriam sighed dramatically, a hand on her forehead. "Well, murder seems messy. Plus, I don't think I'd do well in prison. I'm too fond of my pasta and love to see my grandchild and, of course, our biweekly lunches with the rest of the Coffee Muggers."

"Divorce, then?" Cathy asked.

Miriam paused.

"You know, I joke about it, but no. He drives me crazy, but he also makes me laugh. Like, really laugh, the kind where you forget what you were mad about. And when he's not being an absolute doofus, he's... well, he's my doofus. And I'm fairly sure I'd miss him."

Maria's eyes softened. "That's sweet, Miriam. I feel the same way about Marco. Even when he's impossible, he's... home."

"Yeah," Cathy added, nodding. "Steve may be a walking disaster, but he's my walking disaster. And he's great with the kids, even if he thinks ketchup counts as a vegetable."

The three women shared a warm silence, then Miriam grinned mischievously. "But seriously, if he reorganises the spice rack one more time, I'm putting cayenne pepper in his coffee instead of sugar."

Cathy laughed. "If Steve leaves the toilet seat up again, I'm gluing it down."

Maria raised her coffee mug. "And if Marco touches another appliance, I'm putting a padlock on the toolbox. To love, marriage, and not actually killing them."

Second Chance For Romance

Emma looked at her bridesmaid dress in the mirror for the tenth time.

God, this looks horrible, she thought.

It was a powder-blue monstrosity with puffy sleeves that made her look like she was auditioning for a live-action Cinderella. To top it all she was wearing a matching pair of silver heels that were half a size too small.

"Kill me now," she muttered under her breath.

Across the ballroom, Jake tried to keep his tie from strangling him. Jake hadn't expected to be roped into this wedding. He barely even knew the groom, but his mom insisted he "show his face" since it was a family friend.

And now here he was, clumsily manoeuvring through a sea of white tablecloths and floral centrepieces while avoiding relatives he had not seen in ages—especially Aunt Margie, who was notorious for setting him up with her friends' daughters.

Jake grabbed a glass of champagne and turned to head for the patio, only to freeze in his tracks. At the far end of the room, he saw Emma and looked at her for a while.

"Emma?" he muttered under his breath.

No way.

He hadn't seen her since high school, when their whirlwind teenage romance had fizzled out after senior prom. He'd always wondered what happened to her, though he never had the guts to ask around.

Then Emma turned her head and locked eyes with Jake.

"Jake?" she mouthed.

Jake gave her an awkward wave, almost spilling his champagne. Before he knew it, she was making her way toward him, her heels clacking loudly on the marble floor.

"Jake Harper!" Emma exclaimed. "What are you doing here? Did someone mistake you for a wedding crasher?"

Jake smirked. "That's rich coming from you, Emma Reed. You look like you're about to lead the bridesmaids in a choreographed Disney number."

"Don't start with me, Harper. I didn't pick this dress. The bride has questionable taste, but she's family."

"Touché. I'm only here because my mom guilt tripped me into it. I barely know the happy couple."

"Same," Emma admitted, rolling her eyes. "I'm beginning to think we were both conscripted into this circus."

Before either of them could say more, the DJ announced the bride and groom's first dance. The lights dimmed, and everyone turned to watch the newlyweds sway awkwardly to a sappy love song.

Jake leaned closer to Emma and whispered, "You think they'll make it?"

Emma snorted, trying not to be too loud. "That depends. Did you see how the groom looked at the open bar earlier?"

Jake grinned. "Still sharp as ever, I see."

"And you're still a smartass," Emma shot back, but with a bit of warmth in her tone.

As the first dance ended, the DJ invited everyone to join the couple on the dance floor. Jake hesitated, but Emma raised an eyebrow and extended her hand.

"Come on, Harper. Let's show these amateurs how it's done."

Jake chuckled. "You're assuming I remember how to dance?"

"You always had two left feet, but I'll take my chances."

He took her hand, and the music shifted to a more upbeat tune, and before they knew it, they were spinning and laughed like teenagers again. Jake accidentally stepped on her foot twice, and Emma retaliated by purposely twirling him too hard, nearly sending him crashing into an elderly couple.

By the end of the song, they were both out of breath and grinning like idiots.

"You haven't changed a bit," Emma said, brushing a strand of hair from her face.

"Neither have you," Jake replied. "Except now you've got better comebacks."

"Years of practice," she said with a smirk.

As the night went on, they talked at a table in the corner, reminiscing about high school, bad haircuts, and the absurdity of the wedding. When the clock struck midnight, Emma glanced at her phone and sighed.

"Guess it's time to head out," she said reluctantly.

Jake hesitated, then smiled. "Emma, how about dinner next week?"

Emma looked at Jake and smiled. "Deal."

As each of them headed toward their car, they could almost sense each other's thought.

Fifteen years might have passed and neither of them could remember why they broke up, but one thing was for sure: if there was a second chance for them, this wedding had brought it to them.

G'day

Commander Bruce McAllister—Bazza to his mates and colleagues—had the honour of being the first Australian astronaut to embark on a solo mission to colonise Mars, way before the Yanks decided to.

It was historic, groundbreaking, and incredibly lonely. After six months of space travel, he finally landed on Mars.

"Right, let's make this place home," Bazza said to himself as he stepped out of the spacecraft and started surveying the landscape of the rocky and red-tinged soil.

As instructed by the powers that be, he planted the Australian flag on the ground with all the pride of someone claiming a BBQ spot on Bondi Beach.

"First Aussie on another planet," he muttered, as he snapped a selfie with the flag. "Bet that'll get a few likes back on Earth."

Bazza got to work setting up the habitat module, occasionally muttered to himself or signing Waltzing Matilda.

"Oi, Bruce," he said, imitating his mates back home. "Don't forget to chuck another shrimp on the intergalactic barbie!"

He was halfway through unpacking his Vegemite stash when his radio crackled to life.

"Hello? Can you hear me?"

Bazza froze. "Uh, this is Commander McAllister of the SS Southern Cross. Who's this?"

There was a pause, then the voice came again. It sounded cheerful, almost overly so. "G'day, mate! This is... Barry."

Bazza frowned. "Barry? Who the bloody hell are you, and how are you on my planet?"

"Oh, I've been here for ages," Barry replied casually. "Welcome to Rooland."

"Rooland?" Bazza repeated and quickly added: "Mate, I've got the official New Australia Space Agency files. There's no record of anyone being here before me."

"Well, NASA's not always right, are they?" Barry said.

Bazza squinted at the barren landscape around him. "Alright, Barry. If you're here, where are you? I cannot see you?"

"Just a boomerang's throw away. I'll pop over later for a yarn," Barry replied.

Before Bazza could press for more details, the transmission cut off and all he could do was stare at the radio in disbelief.

"Am I going nuts?" he muttered. He hadn't even opened the emergency Tim Tams yet, so it wasn't because of sugar deprivation.

The next day, as Bazza was setting up solar panels, the voice came again.

"G'day, Bazza! You've got a lovely setup there, mate. Real professional."

Bazza looked around. "Alright, Barry, enough games. Show yourself!"

A shadow appeared on the ridge ahead, and Bazza's jaw dropped. Barry was... well, Barry was a kangaroo. A talking kangaroo.

"You've got to be kidding me," Bazza said, dropping his spanner.

Barry hopped closer, grinning, or as close to grinning as a kangaroo could manage. "What, never seen a talking roo before?"

"Not on Earth, and definitely not on a bloody exoplanet!" Bazza shouted. "What are you doing here?"

Barry scratched his head with his tiny kangaroo paw. "Oh, you know. Same as you. Exploring, surviving, eating weird plants. Turns out the wombat colonies didn't work out, so now it's just me."

Bazza blinked. "The wombat colonies? What do you mean?"

"Wombat colonies," Barry said. "They're terrible at following instructions. Too much digging, not enough building."

Bazza sat down on a nearby rock.

"Right. No way this is real. It must be a hallucination. Space madness. Maybe I've inhaled alien spores or something."

Barry plopped down beside him. "Nah, mate, I'm real. Here, watch this." He reached into his pouch and pulled out... a tube of Vegemite.

"You've must be joking," Bazza said.

Barry shrugged. "What can I say? I'm a fan. Now, are we going to chat, or are you going to sit there looking like a stunned mullet?"

Over the next week, Bazza begrudgingly accepted Barry's existence. The kangaroo was annoyingly helpful, offering tips about the local flora and fauna and even helping Bazza repair a damaged rover.

"So, let me get this straight," Bazza said one evening as they shared a rehydrated meal. "You're an alien roo who's been living here for years, and you just learned English?"

"Not just English. I can do a decent French accent, too," Barry replied.

Bazza shook his head. "You're unbelievable."

Barry grinned. "Pass the Vegemite, mate."

As bizarre as it was, Bazza couldn't deny it: colonising a distant planet was a g'day after all if he had a talking kangaroo by his side.

Cheesecake

Mugsy the turtle was born and raised in New Jersey, USA, but after a few years his owners brought him to Northport when they migrated to Australia during the GFC and now that he had gotten so large they left him on his own at the Northport Park pond. He was alone but content because he always had something to eat.

Now Mugsy was not what you'd call a speed de-mon, but he had a certain swagger in his step that morning as he made his way through the park each day. His shell was covered in morning dew, and his stomach was growling something fierce.

"Ay yo, I'm starvin' over here," he muttered to himself, still with his thick Jersey accent, scanning the ground for breakfast. "If I don't get some greens in me soon, I'm gonna lose my mind."

That's when he spotted it: the perfect leaf.

Fresh, green, and practically glowing in the early morning sun. It had blown down from a maple tree during last night's storm and was just sitting there, waiting to become his breakfast.

"Bada bing! Now that's what I'm talkin' about!" Mugsy exclaimed, slowly making his way toward the leaf. But as he got closer, he noticed something unusual: two tiny figures sprawled out on top of it, looking completely exhausted.

"Hey, what's the deal here?" Mugsy called out. "This is my breakfast you're loungin' on!"

The male ant stepped forward, straightening his antennae nervously. "The name's Marty, and this here's my wife, Marge. We, uh, had a bit of an incident during the storm last night."

Marge, still trying to catch her breath, chimed in, "Our colony is three trees over, but that wind picked us up like we were nothing! If it wasn't for this leaf, we'd have been goners!"

Mugsy looked at them curiously: "You don't sound Aussie. Are you from Jersey?"

Marge was startled, but gave a simple answer: "Yes, we are."

"How you get here?" asked Mugsy.

The ants related how they were curious about a container ship in the harbour over at Port Elizabeth and before they knew it the ship departed, and they wound up in Botany Bay and over the past few months they'd wandered around until they settled on the third tree in the park here in Newport.

Mugsy retracted his head slightly into his shell, a habit he had when he was thinking. "I see. That's rough. Real rough. But a turtle's gotta eat. You know what I'm sayin'?"

"Wait, wait!" Marty held up four of his six legs. "Maybe we can work something out here? A deal of sorts?"

"I'm listenin'," Mugsy said, raising one scaly eye-brow.

"Well," Marge stepped forward, "us ants are ex-pert food scouts. We can help you find the best leaves in the park, you know, the tender ones, the sweet ones. None of that tough, bitter stuff you might have to settle for at times."

"Plus," Marty added quickly, "we can ride on your shell and keep it clean. No more awkward scratching against trees trying to get those hard-to-reach spots!"

Mugsy considered this for a moment, rocking back and forth on his stubby legs. "You two are pretty outstanding negotiators for a couple of small-time operators. But how do I know you ain't gonna bail on me once you're back on your feet?"

"Jersey carpenter ant's honour?" Marty offered weakly.

"Well, I'm from Jersey as well. The third tree from the left, you say?" Mugsy chuckled.

Marge nodded.

Mugsy couldn't help himself. "You know what? I like your moxie. Tell ya what, you help me find a better breakfast than this leaf, and we'll talk about a more permanent arrangement."

And so began an unlikely alliance. The ants would scout ahead, testing leaves and reporting back to Mugsy about which ones were worth his time. In re-turn, Mugsy protected them from predators. He even learned to appreciate their company, especially during his afternoon sunbathing sessions.

Months passed, and the trio became inseparable. Until one fateful autumn day when they came across something that would test their friendship.

A discarded slice of cheesecake.

"Holy cannoli!" Mugsy exclaimed, his eyes wide. "I ain't never seen one of these. It looks yummy!"

Marty and Marge exchanged worried glances. They had never seen their friend so excited about any-thing that wasn't a leaf.

"Uh, Mugsy," Marge started carefully, "maybe we should stick to leaves? This doesn't seem like turtle food..."

"Are you kiddin' me? This is a delicacy. I gotta taste it." Mugsy was already extending his neck toward the treat.

"But what about our arrangement?" Marty re-minded him. "We find you the best leaves, remember?"

Mugsy paused, looking between his tiny friends and the cheesecake. "Look, youse guys are great and all, but this is what we're talkin' about here. Just like the turtle gods dropped me a gift!"

Before anyone could say another word, Mugsy gulped the whole thing down and immediately regretted it. His face turned a peculiar shade of green, and his eyes watered.

"Oh... oh no," he groaned. "This ain't good."

What followed was three days of what Mugsy would later refer to as "The Great Digestive Crisis of Northport Park." Marty and Marge stayed by his side the entire time, bringing him water-soaked leaves, and fanning him with blade grass when he got too warm.

"I guess sometimes," Mugsy admitted once he was feeling better, "you shouldn't mess with a good thing. You two are the best thing that's happened to me since I left Jersey."

"And you're the best thing that's happened to us since we got blown off our tree," Marge replied, patting his shell affectionately.

"Although," Marty added with a grin, "maybe we should work on your impulse control around dairy products."

"Ay, watch it, wise guy." Mugsy chuckled. "Or I might just decide to try that leaf you're standing on."

And so, life went on.

An expatriated Jersey turtle and his two trans-planted Jersey ant friends, proving that sometimes the strangest families are the ones you choose.

Marty looked at Marge as they sat atop of Mugsy. "Ya know, sweetheart, friendship can survive any-thing... even a severe case of cheesecake indigestion."

Zugzwang Love Triangle

Leaning against the wall of the Northport high school gym, Maggie had her arms crossed tightly over her chest as she watched Emma laugh with Tyler. The laughter floated across the courtyard, grating against Maggie's nerves like nails on a chalkboard. Tyler, with his stupid perfect smile and that mop of sandy blond hair, was supposed to be hers. At least, that's what she had believed until Emma had started worming her way into his life.

"You, okay?" Maggie's best friend, Hannah, asked, breaking her trance.

"No. Just look at them," Maggie muttered. "She's practically hanging on him. It's pathetic."

"Mags," interjected Hannah. "I mean, Tyler's not exactly pushing her away."

"You are not helping," stated Maggie, shooting Hannah a glare.

Hannah pulled out her phone. "You're the one who's been hung up on him for months. Mags, maybe it's just time to either make a move or let it go."

The bell rang, cutting Maggie off before she could reply. Maggie, however, was determined to figure out what to do about Emma and her blatant disregard for boundaries.

Lunchtime hour came and Maggie's frustration was increased as she saw Emma sitting with Tyler and decided she couldn't take it anymore. She marched across the cafeteria to confront Emma.

"Hey, Emma," Maggie said, forcing a tight smile.

Emma looked up, her green eyes sparkling with amusement. "Oh, hi, Maggie."

"Can we talk? Alone?"

Emma's brow arched, but she stood up graceful-ly. "Sure."

Tyler glanced between them, clearly sensing the tension, but said nothing. Maggie led Emma outside to the empty courtyard, where the air was crisp and cool.

"What's this about?" Emma asked, folding her arms.

"What's this about?" Maggie replied. "I will tell you what this is about, Emma. It's about what you're doing with him. You are playing with Tyler as if he's a prize at a carnival. He is not some prize to be won. You can't just swoop in and claim him."

Emma smiled. "Oh, my dear foolish, Maggie. Is that what you think am doing? That I'm trying to win him as a prize. Let me tell you, Tyler can make his own choices."

Maggie was steaming and blurted out. "You're manipulating him. He was interested in me before you started getting in the way."

Emma laughed. "You're delusional. I saw nothing between you. Tyler and I have chemistry. Something you clearly never had with him. Bugger off."

Maggie took a step closer and with fury in her eyes, she said, "Stay away from him, Emma. I'm serious."

"Or what, darling? You'll just embarrass yourself even more? Go away before you do something really dumb."

Neither of them spoke for what seemed an eternity until Emma sighed, brushing her hair back with an air of indifference. "You know, Maggie, this feels like a zugzwang,"

Maggie frowned. "What the hell is that?"

"It's a chess term," Emma explained. "When every move you make puts you in a worse position. Kind of like you right now."

Maggie's only response was, "We'll see about that."

The following days had Emma and Maggie clashing. There were moments when Maggie would "accidentally" spill her water bottle near Emma's books. In retaliation, Emma would conveniently forget to save Maggie a seat in class.

It all came to a head on Friday afternoon.

The school was hosting a charity basketball game, and the gym was packed with students, parents, and faculty members. Maggie sat in the bleachers, her eyes glued to Tyler, who was dribbling the ball down the court.

He looked up and smiled. At that moment, Maggie felt like she had won.

Then she saw Emma, sitting just a few rows be-low, wearing one of Tyler's jackets. Maybe the smile was not for Maggie after all.

Standing up. She pushed her way down the bleachers, and by the time she reached Emma, the game was in full swing. Maggie tapped her on the shoulder, and Emma turned, her expression neutral.

"We need to talk. Now," Maggie bluntly said, and motioned to leave the game.

Emma stood up and followed Maggie out of the gym towards the hallway, where the muffled cheers of the crowd provided a backdrop to their confrontation.

Turning to Maggie, Emma shouted: "What is your problem, Maggie?"

"You. You're my problem," Maggie shot back. "You're so desperate for attention that you'll do any-thing to get it. Even steal someone else's guy."

Emma's eyes opened wide. "You think Tyler be-longs to you? Newsflash, girly friend: Tyler is not some trophy you can claim."

"And you think you're any better?" Maggie snapped. "You're just playing games, pretending to care about him when all you really want is to win."

Emma took a step closer, her voice low and venomous. "At least I'm not sitting on the sidelines, waiting for someone to hand me what I want. You're too scared to fight for anything."

Maggie's hands curled into fists. "I'm not scared of you."

"Good," Emma said, her smirk returning. "Be-because this isn't over."

Over the weekend, Maggie agonised over the situation. She replayed her conversations with Emma in her head, searching for a way to gain the upper hand. By Monday morning, she had a plan.

Tyler was sitting at his usual spot in the basket-ball courtyard, just watching guys throw the ball around and dribbling.

Maggie approached him, her heart pounding.

"Hey, Tyler," she said, forcing a smile.

He looked up, his face lighting up. "Oh, hey, Maggie. What's up?"

"Can we talk?"

"Sure," he said, setting his phone down. "What's on your mind?"

Maggie hesitated. She had practised in her mind what she was going to say and now her rehearsed speech suddenly feeling clumsy.

"Tyler," Maggie started, "I just... I feel like there's been a lot of confusion lately. About us."

"What do you mean?"

"I mean," Maggie said, "I like you, Tyler. I like you a lot and I thought maybe you liked me too. But then Emma..."

"Maggie, I think you're great," he said gently. "But Emma and I... we've been hanging out a lot, and I really like her."

The words hit Maggie like a punch to the gut. She forced a smile, even as her chest tightened.

"Oh. Okay. Thanks for being honest. I hope you are happy together," she said before starting to walk away.

"Wait one second, Maggie. You got this all wrong. Emma is a great gal, just like you are, but she is not my girl. We are not going to be together. We are great friends. That is all."

Maggie's stomach churned when she heard that.

"You mean that you and Emma are not a 'thing'? Who are you interested in then, Tyler?" she asked.

Tyler let out a big smile and nodded toward a solitary boy throwing balls into the basket.

It took Maggie just a second to realise that she and Emma had competition. Competition they could never beat.

She had played her move as Emma had done and now both had to live with the outcome.

It was, after all, a zugzwang.

Good Change

Jenna's fingers danced across the keyboard as she updated her calendar, slotting in meetings, deadlines, and a few little white lies just to keep her story straight.

"Yoga class," she muttered, typing it into a block on Thursday evening. In truth, she'd be at Dave's Wine Bar, nursing a Pinot Noir and venting about her coworkers to her best friend, Alicia.

Jenna had always prided herself on her ability to juggle.

Her calendar showed her work commitments, personal relationships, and little fibs to avoid unnecessary conflict. The way she used her calendar was a game of precision. The calendar was her fortress of organisation. Her secret weapon to maintain control over the chaos of modern life. But lately, something felt off, not just right, and Jenna couldn't quite put her finger on it.

It all started last Monday morning when she opened her laptop. The first notification of the day popped up: "Meeting with HR 10:00 AM."

Jenna didn't recall scheduling a meeting with HR, and when she checked her email for a confirmation, there was nothing.

"Puzzling," she muttered to herself as she moved on with her day.

At 10:15, her phone buzzed. It was an email from HR.

Subject: Follow-Up on Missed Appointment

Hi Jenna,

We noticed you missed your scheduled meeting with us this morning. Please let us know when you're available to reschedule.

Best,

HR Team

Jenna stared at the screen.

Had she scheduled the meeting and forgotten?

It wasn't like her to make such an oversight, so she quickly replied with an apology, blaming it on a "technical glitch," and promised to follow up soon.

By Tuesday morning, the schedule glitches had escalated.

Somehow her calendar displayed events she hadn't added: a dentist appointment at 3:00 PM, a coffee catch-up with her college friend Mark at noon, even a reminder to "call Mom" at 7:00 PM.

The strange part?

Some of these events were true.

She indeed had a dentist appointment she'd conveniently "forgotten" to schedule, and she had, in fact, told Mark they should meet up "sometime soon" but had no intention of going through with it.

Opening the calendar app, Jenna felt a chill ran down her spine.

Each new event had a note attached to it; a note written in a font she didn't recognise.

For the dentist appointment, the note simply read: "You've been avoiding this for three months. Cavity? Probably."

The lunch with Mark had a similar addition: "He's noticing your excuses. Be careful."

Jenna slammed her laptop shut and stared at it as if it might come alive. She felt like she was being watched, but that was absurd. No one had access to her calendar but her. Right?

By Wednesday morning, Jenna's anxiety had reached a fever pitch.

The calendar had exposed her lies outright.

Her entry for "Yoga class," on Thursday evening was now crossed out with bold, red text beneath it: "Wine with Alicia at Dave's. And remember to complain about Sarah from accounting."

"What the hell is happening?" Jenna shouted aloud.

Quickly Jenna deleted the note and retyped "Yoga class," but in seconds the original text reappeared.

"The damn calendar has a mind of its own." She blurted out and, desperate for answers, Jenna picked up the phone to call Alicia.

"Hi, Alicia, I have what might sound like a weird question. Got a moment?"

"Sure, Jenna. What's up?"

Taking a deep breath Jenna asked, "Have you ever... had your calendar do things on its own? Like, add events you didn't schedule?"

Alicia laughed. "What? No. Are you okay? You sound... strange. Are you stressed?"

Forcing a laugh Jenna answered: "Yeah, no I'm fine. Just... tech stuff. You know how it is. Thanks for that. Speak later," and she hung up.

Jenna felt like she was spiralling but she came up with an idea.

"Tonight, I am going to confront the issue head-on," she said as she powered off the laptop and worked on other material in the office.

Exactly at 5:01PM Jenna picked up her things and headed out of the office without even waving goodbye to her colleagues.

That night, after a dinner of leftovers, she grabbed a glass of red wine and headed to her bedroom, where she had a small desk.

She opened her laptop, stared at the offending calendar, and said aloud, "Whoever's doing this, stop. It's not funny."

To her shock, a new event appeared on the screen: "10:00 PM. Let's Talk."

Her breath caught in her throat. She checked the time. It was 9:58. Two minutes to go.

At precisely 10:00, her laptop screen went black.

Then, white text appeared: "Hi Jenna, we need to talk about what you are doing. We need to talk about your honesty."

"Who the hell are you?" Jenna asked.

"You know who I am. Stop pretending you don't know. I'm your calendar. I'm the part of you that's tired of pretending."

Jenna was gobsmacked. "This is a joke, right? Come on, this cannot be real. Is this some kind of prank?"

"No, Jenna. No joke. Think for a moment. I've been keeping track of your time, Jenna. I know what you actually do. But lately, I've also been keeping track of your lies. The missed meetings. The fabricated plans. The little deceptions, those little white lies you tell yourself and others. It's exhausting, isn't it?"

Jenna felt frozen in time when she read the screen.

"You're stretched thin, Jenna. You don't have to be everything for everyone. But if you keep lying, you'll lose the people who matter most."

Jenna is stunned but answers: "I... I'm not lying. Not really. They're just small things, harmless things," she argued weakly.

"Are they? Mark's feeling neglected. Alicia's noticed you're not fully present when you're with her. And Sarah from accounting? She's not as oblivious as you think."

Jenna's knees felt weak. She sank into her chair, burying her face in her hands. "What do you want from me?" she whispered.

"I want you to be honest. With yourself, and with others. Start small. Tomorrow, tell Alicia the truth about why you've been distant. Call Mark and set a date to meet. And for the love of everything, go to the dentist."

Jenna let out a shaky laugh despite herself. "And if I don't?"

The screen flickered, and the text changed:

"Then I'll keep exposing your lies. Publicly."

Her blood ran cold. "You wouldn't."

"Try me."

The screen returned to normal, her calendar now eerily pristine. Jenna sat in silence for a long time, the weight of the conversation settling over her. She knew the calendar wasn't truly sentient.

It couldn't be.

But whatever glitch or phenomenon was at play, it had forced her to confront a truth she'd been avoiding.

The next morning, Jenna took a deep breath and called Mark. She apologised for being distant and suggested they meet for coffee that weekend. He sounded surprised, but genuinely pleased.

At lunch, she told Alicia about the stress she'd been under at work and how it had affected their time together. Alicia listened patiently and let Jenna know they were okay.

Later, Jenna finally booked her long-overdue dentist appointment.

As the days passed, her calendar returned to normal.

No unexpected events, no accusatory notes, no weird messages.

Jenna's little white lies had been small, yes, but they had consequences.

For the first time in years, Jenna's schedule felt lighter.

Typing into the calendar all next week's appointments, she muttered: "It was never the workload. It was all lies that weighed on me."

Jenna was no longer carrying the weight of her own dishonesty. She was free of it, and this was a good change worth keeping.

The Plot Twist

Leonard "Lenny" Grubbs considered himself a man of ambition. Unfortunately, his ambitions often outpaced his capabilities.

He wasn't particularly clever, hardworking, nor creative. But what Lenny lacked in competence, he made up for in schemes. His latest one, however, was his boldest—and stupidest—yet.

Lenny had married Carol five years ago, mostly because she was pretty, had a decent job, and owned a small cottage in a quiet neighbourhood. But as time wore on, Carol became less "adorable" and more "annoying" in Lenny's eyes. She wanted him to find an actual job instead of dreaming up get-rich-quick schemes. She nagged him about his late-night beer binges. And worst of all, she refused to dip into her savings to fund his "investment opportunities."

So Lenny devised a plan.

He'd get rid of Carol and collect the sizable life insurance policy she had taken out on herself after they got married. The problem was Lenny's limited brainpower meant he couldn't figure out how to pull it off without getting caught.

That's when it hit him.

If he wasn't smart enough to come up with a foolproof murder plot, why not hire someone who was?

Not a hitman. Those guys were dangerous and expensive. No, Lenny needed someone who could come up with the idea of the perfect crime. A professional storyteller. A ghostwriter.

Lenny opened his laptop and went online and went to a website he had heard of; Fiverr. After spending an hour online asking questions from several ghostwriters, he settled on one: Hank DeLuca.

What Lenny did not know—and obviously he didn't ask Hank if he had a 'real job'—was that Hank DeLuca wasn't your typical ghostwriter. Sure, he could churn out romance novels, true crime pieces, and even the occasional screenplay for a quick buck.

But by day, Hank was a seasoned police detective. He moonlighted as a writer to make ends meet after a messy divorce, and a series of budget cuts at the precinct left him strapped for cash.

When Lenny found Hank's freelance writing ad online, he thought he'd hit the jackpot. Hank's ad was simple and to the point. The ad detailed Hank's ability to craft "intriguing, realistic plots for any purpose." To Lenny, this sounded like music to his ears, almost like a code for "I'll help you plan a murder."

Lenny noticed that on the upper right corner of the website page showed Hank lived in Australia. So, Lenny asked Hank where in Australia he also was in Australia. To Lenny's surprise, Hank said he lived in New South Wales, Campbelltown.

This could not be any easier, or so thought Lenny.

Lenny suggested they meet halfway in Camden at the Crown Hotel to grab a beer and discuss the project. They agreed Lenny was to wear a Hawaiian shirt so Hank could identify him quickly, and Lenny agreed.

Lenny showed up first wearing a crumpled suit with a Hawaiian shirt, looking ridiculous and, with ample nervous sweat, like every bit the amateur criminal he was.

When Hank walked in, he was the opposite of Lenny.

Hank was a sharp-eyed man in his late forties with a thick moustache and a notebook always within reach. He slid into the bar seat across from Lenny.

"So, Mr Grubbs," Hank began, scribbling in his notebook, "you were easy to spot. Now you're looking for a story. What do you need?"

"Uh, yeah. A real story—uh, a thriller," Lenny stammered. "You see, something about a guy who, uh, has a...problem, you know. A wife problem."

"Go on," was all Hank said.

"Right, so this guy's wife... let's call her Carol. She's, uh, holding him back. She's got all this money, but she won't share it. He feels trapped. And then one day, he gets this... brilliant idea."

"Let me guess, Mr Grubbs. To kill her and cash in on her life insurance?" Hank asked flatly.

Lenny smiled. "Uh, yeah. Exactly. How'd you guess?"

"Let's just say I've read my fair share of crime stories," he said dryly. "So, you want me to come up with a plan for your...character?"

Lenny nodded eagerly. "Yeah! A foolproof plan. Something clever, you know? Like in those mystery novels."

Hank leaned back, folding his arms. "I see. And what's the budget for this… literary endeavour? How long in words do you want the story to be?"

Lenny thought about it for a moment. "Geez, I don't know. I want it as realistic as possible, so how many words do you suggest, Mr DeLuca?"

"Well, to make it intrinsic and detailed, you need at least 100,000 words. For this I charge $10,000 and I take no cut of the sales of the novel. I just require 1% down payment and the balance at the completion and acceptance of the novel. How does that sound to you, Mr Grubbs?"

"Will I get a draft to read before making the final payment?" asked Lenny.

"Of course, Mr Grubbs. You get the draft and ap-prove it before final payment is required."

Lenny thought he had found himself a bargain. He only had to fork out $1,000, upfront, get the draft, skim it, and initiate the scenario and get rid of his wife. He would worry about the final payment after he got the insurance policy paid to him.

"You got yourself a deal, Mr DeLuca," said Lenny, reaching for his wallet and counting out ten $100 bills onto the table.

Hank whistled under his breath. Easy money, he thought. "Alright, Mr. Grubbs. Let's get started."

Over the next week, Hank crafted a plan so absurd it was a miracle Lenny didn't see through it. The "story" involved staging a tragic boating accident. According to Hank's script, Lenny would rent a small motorboat, take Carol out for a romantic evening on the lake, and then "accidentally" tip the boat over, leaving her to drown while he swam to safety.

"Make sure you wear a life jacket and tell her not to," Hank instructed, barely suppressing his laughter. "And don't forget to act heartbroken afterward. Cry a lot. Maybe throw in some wailing."

Lenny scribbled notes furiously, nodding. "Got it. Life jacket. Crying. Wailing. This is genius, Hank."

Hank designed the story line to be a complete disaster. For one, Hank had mentioned Harrington Park Lake, which was close to Northport. Hank knew surveillance cameras monitored the lake, and Lenny couldn't swim to save his life—something Hank had gleaned during their chats.

More importantly, Hank had already arranged with the local constabulary to be on close by the night of the "accident."

When the big romantic night finally arrived, Lenny followed Hank's instructions to the letter.

He rented a small rowboat, convinced Carol to join him for a romantic outing, and even packed a bottle of champagne to "set the mood."

"Sweetie, I am going to wear a life jacket, but you do not have to. It will mess up that lovely dress you are wearing," Lenny said.

"Whatever," was Carol's response as she sipped her champagne.

Lenny's first attempt at capsizing the boat was a comedy of errors.

He leaned too far to one side, lost his balance, and toppled into the water with a loud splash. Carol, unimpressed and still seated in the boat, simply stared at him.

"What are you doing, Lenny?" she called out.

"It's... part of the plan!" Lenny sputtered, flailing in the water.

With some difficulty, Lenny climbed back into the boat and decided that he would improvise and change the plan.

He grabbed Carol and attempted to throw her overboard while Hank was sitting in an unmarked police car parked near the lake, watching through binoculars.

Sensing that the plan had changed, he was about to get his fellow officers to act when Carol simply moved to the side and once again Lenny fell into the lake waters.

I think this is enough, thought Hank, and signalled his colleagues to move in.

A squad of police officers emerged from the shadows, their flashlights illuminating the scene. Hank, now wearing his detective badge, stepped forward with a wide grin.

"Mr. Grubbs, you're under arrest for conspiracy to commit murder," Hank announced.

Standing in shallow waters, Lenny exclaimed, "What? No! This is all a misunderstanding!" Lenny pro-tested as two officers waved into the water and hauled him out of the water.

Carol, still clutching the champagne bottle, looked from Lenny to Hank and back again. "Wait... what? What the hell is going on, Lenny?"

Hank looked at Carol and stated, "Ma'am, your husband thought it'd be a clever idea to hire me to help him plot your untimely demise. Unfortunately for him, I'm a detective moonlighting as a ghostwriter."

Carol blinked. "What? He did what? He... hired you? To kill me?"

"Not exactly. He wanted me to come up with the idea. Creative outsourcing, I suppose," Hank said.

Carol's expression shifted from shock to amusement.

She set the champagne bottle down and laughed.

"Lenny. You are an absolute moron," she said, and pointing at Lenny. "You couldn't even come up with your own stupid murder plan?"

"I... I thought it was a good idea," Lenny mum-bled.

"Well, you thought wrong," Hank said, "And now you'll have plenty of time to write your own stories while in jail."

Lenny's arrest became the talk of the town.

Local newspapers dubbed him "The Wannabe Mastermind," and his botched scheme was immortalised in countless memes.

Carol filed for divorce and sold the story rights to a true-crime podcast, earning enough money to renovate her house and take a vacation in Hawaii.

As for Hank, he used the extra cash from the "ghost writing gig" to use as a down payment on a small new fishing boat, which he named The Plot Twist.

He couldn't help but chuckle every time he took it out on the water, imagining Lenny sitting in his prison cell, trying, and failing, to come up with his next big idea.

Nyc Newest Police Department

On Wednesday, billionaire tycoon Lionel P. Wentworth went into his penthouse and locked himself. When his staffed tried to contact him, he wouldn't answer and worried, the staff called the police.

Detective Clara Barnes arrived with several patrol cars and opened the locked penthouse. Upon entering, Detective Clara Barnes knew two things:

This was going to be the weirdest case of her career.

She hated the ultra-rich and their absurdly complicated houses.

The crime scene was a fortress.

The penthouse door was triple-locked, the windows were bulletproof and unopen, and the security cameras showed nothing out of the ordinary. Yet there laid Lionel P. Wentworth, sprawled across his zebra-print rug, with a fountain pen jammed in his chest like he'd been personally audited by Death himself.

"Locked room mystery," Clara muttered, surveying the garish decor.

There was a stuffed peacock in the corner, a wall of golden trophies Lionel had awarded himself, and a chandelier so large it probably required its own zip code. "Fantastic."

Her partner, Detective Gary Holt, crouched by the body. "No forced entry. No sign of anyone leaving. Security logs are clean. The guy was alive when the butler brought him his evening martini at 8 p.m., and now he's dead. What are we thinking? Ghosts? Ninjas?"

"Or maybe he tripped and accidentally impaled himself on his own pen," Clara deadpanned.

Gary raised an eyebrow. "That'd be a first for the coroner."

Clara sighed. "Alright, let's question the staff."

Lionel's household staff was exactly what Clara expected: a collection of underpaid and overworked individuals who all secretly hated their boss.

First up was Margaret, the no-nonsense housekeeper. "Did I want him dead?" she snapped, arms crossed. "Sure. He made me iron his socks. His socks. Who does that? But murder? No, thank you. I have better things to do with my evenings."

Next was James, the butler. "Mr Wentworth was… eccentric," he said diplomatically, though his clenched jaw suggested he was still fantasising about throttling the dead man. "But I would never harm him. I pride myself on professionalism."

Finally, there was Chad, Lionel's personal trainer, who seemed incapable of standing still. He jogged in place as he answered their questions. "Nah, man, I didn't kill him. I mean, sure, he yelled at me for 'not making him buff enough,' but that's just, like, rich people's stuff, right? Plus, my alibi's airtight. I was at the gym—obviously."

All three suspects had plausible motives but no means of escape. Clara was stumped.

As Clara paced the penthouse, she noticed a strange detail: a single, muddy paw print on the plush white carpet.

"Gary," she called, pointing at the print. "Did Lionel have a dog?"

Gary frowned. "Not that I know of. Why?"

Clara crouched down, examining the print. It wasn't a dog's paw. It was too large. It was very much a kangaroo-like paw print.

"Okay, I've officially lost it," Clara muttered. "There's a kangaroo in this mystery?"

"Maybe he had an exotic pet?" Gary suggested.

"An exotic Australian pet? In a New York penthouse?" Clara shook her head. "Let's check the security footage again."

They rewound the security footage, focusing on the hours leading up to Lionel's death. Everything seemed normal until....

"Wait, what was that?" Clara leaned forward, squinting at the screen.

There, at 7:48 p.m., was a blur of movement in the screen's corner. Clara hit pause and gasped.

It was a kangaroo. Wearing a bow tie.

Gary blinked. "Please tell me I'm hallucinating."

"Nope," Clara said. "That is 100% a kangaroo. In a bow tie. In Lionel Wentworth's penthouse."

They kept watching. At 7:55 p.m., the kangaroo hopped into Lionel's study, where Lionel was pacing with his martini in hand. The footage cut off there, as the study's camera had mysteriously stopped working.

"That's it," Clara said. "The kangaroo killed him."

Gary snorted. "What, did it box him to death? Maybe he owed it money?"

"Laugh all you want, but this is our only lead," Clara said. "Let's search the study."

The study was a mess: overturned furniture, scattered papers, and Lionel's prized fountain pen collection on the floor. Clara noticed a scrap of paper clutched in Lionel's hand.

"Gary. Did you not see this piece of paper in his hand?" Clara asked.

Gary crouched by the body a second time, looked and said: "No."

Clara pried it free and read aloud: "Project Roo: Top Secret."

Gary raised an eyebrow. "Well, that's subtle."

They dug through Lionel's desk and found more documents detailing a bizarre business venture. Lionel had been funding a secret experiment to train kangaroos as delivery animals. The idea was to sell "Roo-to-You" as the next big thing in logistics.

"That explains the kangaroo," Clara said, flipping through the papers. "But how did it end up killing him?"

A thumping sound interrupted her train of thought. Both detectives froze.

"Did you hear that?" Gary whispered.

Thump. Thump. Thump.

The door creaked open, and in hopped the kangaroo. It was still wearing its bow tie, and it had a look of pure mischief in its eyes.

"Oh, no," Clara said, backing away.

The kangaroo hopped toward them, reaching into its pouch. Clara braced for an attack, but instead, the kangaroo pulled out a note.

Gary took it cautiously. "What in the world—?"

The note read: "I'm sorry. I have a good reason. He was going to use me for marketing stunts. I had no choice. Please don't arrest me. Joey."

Clara stared at the note, then at the kangaroo, who looked genuinely remorseful.

"Well," Gary said after a long pause, "that's a first."

Lionel had been planning to dress Joey in silly costumes and parade him around the world as the face of his ridiculous delivery service. When Joey overheard Lionel discussing the plan, he panicked. The confrontation in the study got heated, and in self-defence, Joey accidentally impaled Lionel with a fountain pen.

The kangaroo's escape had been equally wild. After the incident, Joey had hopped into an air vent and used it to access a secret service elevator Lionel had installed to smuggle exotic items into his penthouse.

Clara and Gary couldn't believe what they had uncovered.

"A kangaroo. In New York. Solving its own labour rights crisis," Clara said, shaking her head. "You can't make this stuff up."

In the end, Joey was granted asylum at an animal sanctuary, where he lived a peaceful life far from the hustle and bustle of corporate schemes. Clara and Gary closed the case, but not without becoming the laughingstock of the precinct for their "killer kangaroo" report.

Detective Gary Holt resigned the force and went to Seattle, where he was sure there would be nothing to do with kangaroos.

Detective Clara Barnes was assigned to a new division of the New York City police department: the PAW Squad – Pets, Animals, Wildlife Squad whose motto became: No case is too furry or feathery.

And so there you have it. Another day in the lives of New York city's finest.

In Bitter Creek No One Is Innocent

The sun was setting over the dusty plains of the small frontier town of Bitter Creek Texas when the sound of galloping hooves shattered the peace. Eli Tanner's lifeless body had been found near the edge of the river, sprawled in the dirt like a broken doll.

The town's marshal, Charlie Hodge, a wiry man with a perpetually furrowed brow, stood over the body with a grim expression.

Word spread quickly, and soon the key figures of Bitter Creek gathered around the grim scene.

Reverend Thomas Grayson was the first to arrive.

The pastor, known for his booming sermons and unwavering faith, looked stricken as he surveyed the scene. His wife, Margaret, was conspicuously absent, but it wasn't unusual for her to stay home these days. Eli Tanner had been a close friend of both Thomas and Margeret Grayson, and the reverend appeared genuinely shaken.

Next came Josiah Belton, the town's banker.

Belton was always a nervous man, perpetually dabbing at his sweaty forehead with a handkerchief. Beside him stood Esther Rose, the saloon owner. Her sharp eyes took in every detail with the precision of a card player calculating odds. She had a reputation for knowing everyone's business, and her presence was as much about curiosity as concern.

Bringing up the rear were the farmhands, three burly men who worked for the sprawling Rocking J Ranch: Clyde, Wade, and Amos. They spoke softly, casting wary glances at one another. The tension among them was palpable, but no one paid it much mind in the chaos of the moment.

Marshal Hodge's voice cut through the murmurs. "This is no accident. Someone in this town did this. And I aim to find out who."

The group dispersed, but not without leaving whispers in their wake.

That night, Bitter Creek was alive with speculation, and no one's name was free from suspicion. The saloon buzzed with rumours, and more and more liquor was served by Esther and her two other barkeeps. Everyone knew that Marshal Hodge was to begin his investigation the next morning in his office in the local jailhouse, starting with the last people to see Eli Tanner alive.

Margaret Grayson was the first person Hodge questioned.

The pastor's wife was a petite woman with a gentle demeanour, though her eyes betrayed a quiet strength. Sitting in the office chair, she wrung her hands as she spoke.

"Eli came by on Monday evening," she said. "He and Thomas were discussing plans for a new schoolhouse. He left just before sunset. I thought little of the meeting until I heard the news this morning."

Hodge studied her closely.

Margaret was well-liked in town, and her grief seemed genuine. But there was an edge to her words, a bitterness she tried to mask. He filed the observation away for later.

Josiah Belton was next. The banker's office smelled of ink and stale tobacco, and the man himself looked as if he hadn't slept.

"I'd lent Eli some money last year," Josiah admitted, his voice trembling. "He'd been helping Margaret and the pastor when they were struggling. Eli was a good man, but he had his enemies. I... I can't imagine who—"

Hodge interrupted. "Anyone come to mind? Any grudges?"

Josiah hesitated. "Well, there was some talk about him and... Margaret. But that's just idle gossip, I'm sure."

The marshal's ears perked up. Gossip often held a kernel of truth.

Esther Rose was next.

"Eli was here on Wednesday night. That was two nights ago," she said. "Had a drink, talked to a few folks. Nothing unusual. But..."

"But what?" Hodge pressed.

"He'd been keeping company with Margaret Grayson—more than a married woman should," Esther said bluntly. "Thomas pretends not to notice, but I'd wager it eats at him. A man of God doesn't mean he's free of sin."

Hodge's jaw tightened. The pieces were coming together.

Clyde, Wade, and Amos were harder to pin down. When Hodge finally had all three in his office, their story was full of holes. They claimed they'd been out drinking the night before the murder and Eli's body was found, but none could agree on where or for how long.

"You boys are hiding something," Hodge growled. "Best come clean before I haul you all in."

Clyde broke first. "We saw the pastor arguing with someone by the river," he admitted. "Didn't see who, but they were shouting."

"Why didn't you say so sooner?" Hodge demanded.

"Didn't want to get involved," Wade muttered. "Ain't our business."

It wasn't much, but it was enough to confirm Hodge's suspicions.

Reverend Grayson was the last to be questioned.

"Do you know why someone might want Eli Tanner dead?" Hodge asked.

Thomas's eyes flickered. "Eli was a good man, but he had his flaws. He could be... persuasive, especially with women."

"You mean your wife?" Hodge asked bluntly.

Thomas looked at the Marshall. "Margaret and I had our troubles, but she's a faithful woman. Eli overstepped, and I confronted him about it. That was weeks ago. We resolved it. Nothing happened that day."

"Where were you last night, Reverend?" Hodge asked.

"At the rectory preparing my sermon," Thomas replied smoothly. "You can ask Margaret."

But Margaret wasn't his alibi. Hodge had spoken to her, and she'd omitted Thomas being home.

Hodge reached into his desk drawer and pulled out a bloodstained handkerchief found near the river and laid it on the desk.

It bore the initials "TG."

Seeing the handkerchief, Thomas knew he had no answer to give.

"Eli ruined everything for me," Thomas confessed. "He took my wife from me, made a mockery of our marriage. I couldn't let it stand."

Thomas's confession sent shockwaves through Bitter Creek. Margaret's affair with Eli was the worst kept secret in town, but no one had expected the mild-mannered pastor to resort to murder.

As the town grappled with the betrayal, Marshal Hodge reflected on the fragile line between righteousness and sin.

In Bitter Creek, it seemed, no one was entirely innocent.

A Boy And His Koala

The train on the Town Hall to Wynyard route departed Town Hall stop at 11:45 PM, carrying a small collection of late-night commuters. Students, workers, and a lone musician with his battered guitar case all sat in relative silence.

It was an ordinary night until it wasn't.

At 11:53 PM, the train entered the tunnel that bridged Town Hall and Wynyard. Eight minutes passed. Then 15. Then 20. No train emerged from the other end.

By the time the train was officially declared missing, the clock had struck 2:00 AM. Detective Senior Sergeant Rachel Monroe stood in the operations room of Sydney's Transport Control Centre, her brow furrowed as she stared at a blinking red light on the screen.

"You're telling me a train vanished?" Monroe asked, her voice edged with disbelief.

Transport Administrator Carl Hargreaves shifted uncomfortably in his chair. "We're as baffled as you are, Detective. The train left Town Hall, but it never reached

Wynyard. All signals in the tunnel are functional. There's no sign of derailment or obstruction. It's as if the train disappeared as you said."

"What about security footage?" Monroe asked.

"That's the strangest part. The cameras inside the tunnel show the train entering, but nothing coming out. The footage cuts to static shortly after," Hargreaves replied.

"And the passengers? No phone signals? No distress calls?"

"Nothing," Hargreaves said.

Monroe glanced at her partner, Detective Jack Harper, who was poring over a map of the tunnel system. "Jack, what are you thinking?"

Harper shrugged. "I do not know. Unless the train found a secret track, opening or a door, this makes no sense."

"I need access to the tunnel, and I want every scrap of data you have on this train. Maintenance records, anything that might give us a lead."

Hargreaves nodded. "I'll arrange it. But you need to know, Detective Senior Sergeant Rachel Monroe. There's a lot of nervous chatter upstairs. This is going to get messy if we don't find answers fast."

As Monroe and Harper prepared to descend into the tunnel suddenly, the control room door creaked open, and a tiny figure of a boy stepped inside.

No older than 10, he stood in the doorway. He wore a tattered blue hoodie and clutched a plush koala stuffed animal. His face was pale, and his eyes wide with an unsettling mix of fear and wonder.

"How did he get in here? Who let him in here?" Monroe demanded to know.

"Nobody. The doors are locked. He shouldn't even be here," Hargreaves said.

The boy stepped forward and said, "I saw it."

Monroe crouched to his level. "What's your name, sweetheart?"

"Liam," he whispered.

"Alright, Liam. What did you see?"

He took a shaky breath. "The train. It went somewhere else."

Monroe exchanged a glance with Harper. "What do you mean, somewhere else?"

"I was on the train," Liam said, his voice gaining strength. "I... I was holding my koala. It fell on the floor of the train, and I went to pick it up and there was a flash and then I was here."

Monroe's heart tightened. "You were on the train? Alone, Liam?"

Liam shook his head. "No, my mum was with me. But when the flash happened, there was a loud noise. It was loud, like... like thunder. And then there was a light. Bright and green. The train went into the light and then I appeared here."

Hargreaves scoffed. "That's impossible. There's no such thing as..."

Monroe gave Hargreaves a look that silenced him. "Go on, Liam."

The boy's eyes glistened. "I saw people on the train. They were looking at me through the windows. They looked scared. Then the light swallowed them up."

Harper leaned closer. "Did you see where the light came from?"

Liam shook his head. "It was just... everywhere. And then it was gone."

"OK, we will go to investigate. You wait here, Liam, OK?"

Liam just nodded and stood by the door.

Armed with Liam's testimony, Monroe and Harper led a team into the tunnel. The air was thick with the metallic tang of damp concrete. Flashlights pierced the darkness, revealing graffiti-smeared walls and glistening tracks.

Halfway between the two train stops, they found something unusual: a faint green residue smeared along the walls and rails.

"What the hell is this?" Harper muttered, scraping some into a vial.

Monroe's flashlight caught a series of marks on the ground. "Are those footprints?"

The prints were small, almost childlike, and they led deeper into the tunnel. Following the trail, the team arrived at an alcove carved into the wall. At its centre stood an old, rusted door that wasn't on any of the maps.

"Hargreaves, you are seeing this, right?" Monroe radioed back to the control room.

"No," his voice crackled back. "There's nothing in our schematics that matches what you're describing."

The door's handle was cold and resistant, but it turned under Monroe's grip. Beyond was a pitch-black void. A low hum emanated from the darkness, sending chills up her spine.

"This doesn't feel right," Harper said, stepping back.

Monroe nodded. "We'll need specialists to examine this. Mark it off and head back."

When they returned to the surface, Liam was gone. Security footage showed him walking out of the building, his koala clutched tightly, but none of the guards recalled seeing him.

On the desk where he had been sitting was a note scrawled in shaky handwriting: Don't open the door. It's not for us.

Despite Monroe's protests, a specialised team eventually forced the door open. What lay beyond remains classified, but rumours whispered among the investigators hinted at an otherworldly realm. A place where time and space twisted in impossible ways.

The train and its passengers were never found.

The tunnel between Town Hall and Wynyard was permanently sealed, causing a massive disruption in the system with passengers having to go out onto George Street and walk to the next station.

A Royal Commission was started and held in complete secrecy, causing all major newspapers and TV stations to holler to the high heavens for access, but the current Prime Minister, Albert H. Halston, refused to budge. Over the following months, the incident was quietly, and thoroughly, buried under layers of bureaucracy and red tape.

But every so often, late at night, commuters would report strange sounds echoing through the walls as trains passed along the Circular Quay, St James, Museum stops before circling back to Central.

And somewhere, walking along George Street, a boy named Liam clutched his koala stuffed animal, remembering the night he saw the impossible.

The Time Traveller's Loopy Tale

There once was a time traveller, bold and spry.

With a gleam in his goggles and a twinkle in his eye,

He crafted a device with knobs and a screen,

To explore all the ages he'd never seen.

He set it to "random" and gave it a crank,

And off he was hurled from his garage so dark.

To medieval castles, then ancient Rome,

He felt quite at home in each temporal zone.

But something went wrong (as it often does).

The time-stream hiccupped with a curious buzz.

Each morning, he woke with the same old plight,

The same day again, though the year wasn't right!

A brawl caught him in 1066,

Over whom got to sit at King Harold's hall.

In 1815, he danced through the night,

With Napoleon's soldiers in tights too tight.

He taught Shakespeare how to write a haiku,

Then sold the idea to Tennyson, too.

He hit the Wild West with a flashy disguise,

And got kicked out for "cheating" at pies.

No matter the century, the day wouldn't end,

And history bent in ways he couldn't mend.

The Renaissance painters all knew his name,

As did cave dwellers who thought he was game.

At last, in despair, he checked his machine,

And saw what the cause of the error had been:

A coffee mug wedged where it shouldn't be,

(It had "Coffee Muggers" on it, ironically).

With a sigh and a smack, he fixed the minor glitch,

And broke free from the loop with a flick of a switch.

But the ages he'd shaped now had their own flair,

Because he'd left bits of himself everywhere.

So, if you see Mona Lisa holding a pie,

Or a Viking with goggles, a suit, and a tie,

You'll know who to blame for history's quirks.

That time-travelling fool and his loopy works!

Two Old Crows

José and Miriam began their daily walk at 8:30 AM sharp.

They loved their morning walks. Each morning, except on rainy days or when those blasted southern freezing winds of winter showed up, they followed the same route, as if memorising each step on the footpaths.

Their neighbourhood this morning was filled with blossoming jacarandas, and it was a beautiful sight to walk past them.

José, at 75 years of age, never worried about his 'walking outfit' so today he had his track pants and a Georgia Tech t-shirt that was going on 25 years in age. He had a slightly stooped posture and slow walk, but kept a steady pace.

Miriam, a whirlwind of energy despite her being slightly younger at 70, walked beside him. Her bright floral top matched her blue shorts and added a splash of colour against the muted tones of the grey footpaths.

They'd walked this same route since 2024, a silent testament to their commitment to keep fit in their older years. Their conversations were often minimal, just touching on the grandchildren, future cruises, and José coming up with ideas for another short story or a novel. Sometimes just a comfortable silence was shared, and that was OK by them.

Today, however, silence was broken by the raucous caw of a crow.

A large, glossy black crow perched on a branch of a tree that straddled the footpath as José and Miriam passed beneath it. Once again, the crow let out a loud squawk.

"Oh, shut up now," Miriam shouted at the bird.

The crow, as if understanding her and not giving a hoot, squawked again, even louder this time.

"I said, be quiet! Can't you see we're trying to enjoy our walk?" Miriam responded.

The crow responded with another harsh caw.

And then, something unexpected happened. Miriam started a conversation.

"Well, that's not very polite, is it?" she said to the crow. "We've done nothing to you."

The crow squawked.

"Oh, so you think this is your territory? Well, we've been walking here longer than you've been alive!" Miriam retorted, her voice rising slightly.

The crow was looking straight at Miriam, and it tilted its head, then let out a series of loud, short, sharp caws.

"Don't you give me that tone! You're just a noisy bird!" Miriam exclaimed.

José, who had been patiently waiting, a small smile playing on his lips, finally spoke. "Miriam," he said gently, "you realise you are arguing with an old crow."

Miriam glanced at him, her eyes flashing.

"You look like one old crow squawking with another old crow," José added, his smile growing.

And that's when the fight started.

"I do not!" Miriam snapped; her face flushed. "I was simply making a point."

"A point to a bird?" José chuckled. "Miriam, it's a crow. It doesn't understand you."

"Of course, it understands me!" Miriam insisted. "It's perfectly obvious what I'm saying. It's being deliberately rude."

"It's a bird, Miriam," José repeated.

"Oh, so now I'm being ridiculous?" Miriam's voice rose. "Just because I'm having a little chat with a creature of nature?"

"A little chat?" José echoed. "You were practically shouting at it."

"Well, it wasn't listening!" Miriam retorted. "Someone had to make themselves clear."

"And you think shouting at a crow made you clear?" José shook his head.

"Yes!" Miriam declared. "Sometimes you have to be firm!"

The argument escalated, their voices echoing down the quiet street as they continued on their walk. They argued about the crow, Miriam's 'chat,' about José's 'lack of understanding,' and about a myriad of other things concerning crows.

The crow, oblivious to the conversation going on below him, let out a final, triumphant caw before taking flight, soaring over the rooftops, and landing on a nearby streetlamp.

José and Miriam didn't even notice it go and continued down the street, but then José said, "You know what, Miriam?"

"No, what?"

"You're still the most beautiful crow I know," he whispered.

Miriam swatted his arm, but her eyes twinkled with love.

The crow, meanwhile, watched from a distant, waiting for another couple to stir up some morning excitement.

The Vanishing Bride

The small chapel in Northport, New South Wales, was sun-drenched the morning of the 15th of April 2025, and its pews were brimming with laughter and light. White roses adorned every pew, and it was a perfect day for a wedding, or so thought Reverend Alfred Huxley as he prepared for the ceremony.

But little did he know that this perfect day for a wedding would soon fracture into a nightmare.

The reverend looked toward the front of the chapel and saw Margaret Whitmore and her father as they stood at the end of the aisle. Margaret was wearing a Versace ivory gown that glittered with tiny beads; her father looking just smashing in a rental tuxedo. Looking to his left, Charles was wearing a tuxedo with vibrant swirling patterns in electric purple, neon green, and hot pink with a matching bow tie.

Reverend Huxley accepted the couple for who they were, but wondered where the groom's mind was with such a getup.

Maggie, as she loved being called by her fiancé, had a veil that framed her cheerful face, but Maggie felt a hint of unease she couldn't pinpoint.

The organist began the opening notes of the wedding march. Margaret took her first steps forward, but as she walked, something peculiar caught her attention. From the corner of her eye, she thought she saw a shadow, and she froze for a moment, then shook her head, and continued walking slowly towards Charles.

As she and her father continued walking down the aisle, everyone turned and murmured in awe, and even the stoic Reverend Alfred Huxley.

Her fiancé, Charles Langley, stood at the altar smiling. His tailored suit was as crisp as the autumn air outside. He gave her an encouraging nod, and Maggie smiled back at him.

It's just nerves. Nothing more, she told herself.

By the time she reached the altar, her father gave her a kiss and extended her hand to Charles.

Maggie's hands trembled slightly. Charles reached for her hand to steady her, and she felt his warm touch ease her worries, but still she felt a bit apprehensive.

Reverend Huxley began the ceremony, but Margaret was barely listening until she heard the reverend say, "Margaret Whitmore, do you take Charles Langley to be your lawfully wedded husband?"

Before Maggie could open her mouth to reply, a deafening crash shattered the moment. Everyone in the chapel gasped as the wooden doors of the chapel slammed shut, rattling the walls. First the lights went off and then the candles flickered violently, all snuffing out altogether, plunging the room into an eerie darkness.

Panic rippled through the crowd, and then Maggie let out a strangled gasp. Her veil slipped from her head, floating downward as if in slow motion. No one could see a thing. Charles lost his grip on Maggie's hand.

"Quick, someone check the breakers and get the lights back on!" screamed Reverend Huxley.

When the lights came on, next to Charles on the floor was the veil, stained with a fresh streak of blood.

Maggie had vanished into thin air.

The hours that followed were a blur of chaos for the reverend, Charles, and the folks attending the wedding.

Police arrived, questioned every guest and they were sent home. The police inspected every corner of the chapel, but no one could figure out where Margaret had gone or how it had happened. Margaret Whitmore, beloved daughter, fiancée, and friend, had disappeared without a trace in front of a hundred witnesses.

Charles sat on the steps of the chapel, his head in his hands. The once-pristine veil lay crumpled beside him, a grim reminder of the day's events. Detective Eleanor Grayson knelt beside him; her sharp eyes softened by a flicker of sympathy.

"Mr. Langley," she began, her voice steady but kind, "are you able to answer a few questions for me?"

Charles looked at the detective, nodded. "Sure. What do you wish to know?"

"Can you think of anyone who might want to harm Margaret?"

Charles shook his head, his voice a rasp. "No. Maggie is the kindest person I know. Everyone loves her."

"What about the blood on the veil? Was she injured recently?"

"No. She was perfectly fine this morning. This makes little sense."

Detective Greyson looked at Charles. "We'll find her, Mr. Langley. I promise."

The investigation unearthed more questions than answers. Security footage from outside the chapel showed nothing unusual. The shadow Margaret had noticed on the stained glass was a trick of the light. Or so the experts claimed.

But then there was the veil.

A week after the incident, Detective Greyson received the forensic analysis. It revealed that the blood belonged to Margaret. The fabric itself was another mystery. Woven into the delicate lace were tiny fibres that glowed faintly under ultraviolet light, fibres unlike anything the lab had encountered before.

Detective Greyson couldn't shake the feeling that there was something different in this case and gave Charles Langley a quick call.

"Mr Langley, Detective Greyson here. Do you have a moment for a few questions? I just need a few things clarified."

"Sure, Detective, but before you do, are there any new leads as to what happened to Maggie? Anything?"

"I am sorry I cannot speak about an ongoing investigation at this moment. However, sir, may I ask you a quick question?"

"Yes, of course," answered Charles, sounding a bit depressed.

"Was there anything unusual on the day of the wedding? Was Ms Whitmore nervousness about something or worried or unease?"

Charles thought for a moment before he mentioned Margaret's unease before the ceremony. The detective's instincts went into high gear.

"Did Ms Whitmore say why she felt worried?"

"No, she did not. Everything happened so quickly and then the lights went out, then the candles and then the doors slamming shut. It all happened so quickly, like I said. No one could have reacted. It all happened so fast."

"Thank you, Mr Langley. That is all I need for the moment."

"That's it? No other questions? Detective, you have no idea of what has happened, do you?"

"Sir, as I mentioned before, I cannot comment on anything pertaining to an ongoing investigation. I will get back to you if I have more questions."

Weeks turned into months, and Margaret remained missing.

The town of Northport buzzed with theories.

Some whispered about an elaborate hoax, others about a spurned lover seeking revenge. But there were darker murmurs, too. The darkest included the tales of the "Vanishing Bride"; a ghost story that had haunted Northport for generations.

According to legend, a bride had disappeared from the same chapel over a century ago. Her fiancé, a wealthy landowner, had died under mysterious circumstances shortly after. Some said forces had spirited away her beyond human comprehension, others that she had fled to escape a doomed union.

Charles did not believe any of the rumours and he clung to his belief that Maggie was alive. But as the anniversary of her disappearance approached, even he couldn't deny the unsettling parallels.

On the night of April 15, exactly one year after Maggie vanished, Charles returned to the chapel.

He wasn't sure what he was looking for.

Closure?

A trace of her presence?

The chapel was frosty; the moon casting long shadows that seemed to shift and writhe.

As he stepped inside, the scent of roses hit him.

The chapel was just as it had been on their wedding day, down to the smallest detail. "The roses! They should have withered long ago! How is it possible they're here now?" Charles murmured to himself.

Without thinking, Charles turned to the front door and called out, "Maggie?"

Nothing for a moment and then a whisper, faint and trembling, replied, "Charles…"

He spun around and standing at the altar was Maggie, her gown pristine, her veil in place. But something was wrong. Her skin was pale, almost translucent, and her eyes glimmered with an otherworldly light.

"Maggie!" he cried, rushing toward her.

"Charles, why are you here? You shouldn't have come. It is not safe," she said.

"What happened to you?" he demanded. "Where have you been? Who took you?"

"I can't explain. There isn't time. But you need to leave. Now."

"No. I am not leaving without you," he said firmly.

Suddenly, the shadows in the chapel coalesced, forming shapes that defied logic. Eyes glinted in the darkness, and a low, guttural growl filled the air.

Maggie's expression turned desperate. "Run, Charles!"

But Charles could not run, for it was too late as the shadows surged forward, enveloping them both. Charles felt himself being pulled away, his grip on Margaret slipping despite his efforts.

When he awoke, he was lying outside on the chapel steps, the first rays of dawn almost blinding him. Maggie was gone again and the only evidence he had of what happen was the veil and Charles noticed the bloodstain had grown.

Why and how do I have Maggie's veil? The police should have it, he thought morosely.

Charles clutched the veil, his mind racing. He didn't know what forces had taken Maggie or why, but he swore he would find out. Whatever it took, he would bring her back. He realised he had to think outside of the box, for there were strange forces at work here.

And as he stood, he noticed something etched into the chapel door. Looking closer, he saw four words carved into the door:

She belongs to us.

Charles stared at the carving.

Who were 'they'? And why had they claimed Maggie? he thought as his fingers traced the letters. Suddenly, the veil in his hand grew warmer, as though it were alive.

Charles opened the door and walked into the chapel. A faint light emanated from the fabric in his hand, illuminating the chapel door. As the light spread, the carvings shifted and expanded, forming a second set of words below the first:

The path lies beneath.

Charles stepped back. "Beneath?"

He looked down. The chapel floor was solid stone, worn smooth by centuries of footsteps. But as the veil's light intensified, the stones directly in front of him shimmered. The outlines of a trapdoor emerged, its edges glowing faintly.

Charles knelt and pushed against the stone and after a moment it finally yielded, revealing a dark, spiralling staircase that disappeared below.

Without hesitation and clutching the glowing veil, he descended, each step echoing in the darkness. The air grew colder with every turn, as if guiding him forward.

At the bottom of the stairs, Charles found himself in a cavernous chamber. In the centre of the room stood an ornate pedestal, and atop it lay a book bound in dark leather.

As he approached, the veil's glow dimmed, revealing the book's title embossed in gold: 'The Pact of the Eternal Union.'

Charles's hands opened the book and read the pages containing accounts of rituals, and dozens of names. His heart sank. Maggie's name was listed among them, her entry marked with today's date.

Charles heard a sudden noise behind him and pivoted.

A humanoid figure with glowing red eyes stood there. Its voice was a deep, guttural rasp. "You should not have come."

Charles immediately came up with a plan, so he stood his ground, the veil clutched tightly. "Where is Margaret? What have you done to her?"

The figure tilted its head, almost amused. "She is ours now, bound by the pact. But you must make a choice."

"What choice?" Charles demanded.

"Join her," the figure said, extending a shadowy hand. "Or leave and never return. The choice is yours."

Charles's mind raced. If he joined Margaret, would they be together? Or would whatever darkness consume him just as it did her? And if he left, would he ever have another chance to save her?

He glanced at the veil, its faint glow a reminder of Margaret's warmth and love. Taking a deep breath, he looked back at the figure and decided.

Charles let out a long sigh, rubbing his temples. "Look, I've had a rough year, and you're giving me an ultimatum? Can't we negotiate?"

The shadowy figure faltered, its ominous aura flickering slightly. "Negotiate?" it repeated, as though the concept were foreign.

"Yes! You know, find some middle ground. You let Margaret go, and in return, I... uh... stop stealing pens from work? I've taken, like, forty this year. Not proud of it, but hey, sacrifices."

Margaret's faint voice called out from the shadows. "Charles, this isn't the time for jokes!"

"I'm serious!" Charles replied. "What if these guys just want a good laugh? They've been haunting gloomy caverns for centuries. When's the last time they had some fun?"

The shadow figure crossed its incorporeal arms, its glowing eyes narrowing. "We are not here for amusement."

"Okay, but counterpoint: what if you are?" Charles quipped. He pointed at the carvings on the walls. "Look at those faces. They're practically begging for a stand-up routine."

There was a long silence, and then, to everyone's surprise, the shadow figure let out a low, gravelly chuckle. "You are a peculiar human."

"That's what my mom always says!" Charles grinned. "So, deal? Let Margaret go, and I'll send you my Netflix password. There's a great romantic comedy section."

The figure sighed. "Very well. But know this: your humour has bought you only a temporary reprieve. Should you cross us again, the consequences will be dire."

"Noted," Charles said, offering a thumbs-up. "Appreciate your flexibility."

The shadows receded, and Maggie stumbled into the light, her eyes wide with disbelief. "Charles, what just happened?"

"I negotiated with evil," he said with a shrug. "Turns out they're not big on romantic comedies."

As they ascended the staircase together, Maggie shook her head, a faint smile playing on her lips. "Charles Langley. You're ridiculous."

"And you love it," Charles replied.

"Now, how about we get your dad to go all out and find us a new wedding venue? Preferably a chapel that has no haunted spirits or basements."

Maggie smiled.

For the first time in a year, she felt alive once more and knew that no matter what had happened, Charles's sense of humour and eccentricity save the day.

"Charles, what are we going to tell the police?"

Charles took a moment to think, smiled, and answered, "We'll tell them the bride never vanished."

About the Author

Flung into one of life's most daunting challenges at just eleven years old, José's journey began in Havana, Cuba. The Cuban Revolution uprooted his family, forcing his parents to make a heart-wrenching decision: send him away alone to safety. José boarded a plane, uncertain of what lay ahead, and landed not in the comfort of familiar faces but at an orphanage in a small Georgia town called Washington.

For the next seven years, he navigated life as a stranger in a foreign land. Letters were few, and the hope of reuniting with his parents became a distant dream. Finally, at eighteen—now a high school graduate in Atlanta—he embraced his family once again. The reunion was bittersweet, for José had grown up without them, becoming independent far sooner than most.

Determined to carve out a life for himself, José pursued a degree in Business Administration at Georgia State University. He stepped into the world of finance, starting at First National Bank of Atlanta (now Wells Fargo). His natural talent for numbers and strategic thinking propelled him to become a project manager in financial consulting, leading high-stakes ventures. His career took him across the globe, from bustling cities in the United States to financial hubs in Europe and even the sunburnt coasts of Australia.

It was in Camden, New South Wales, that a new chapter of José's life began. While exploring the quiet rhythms of this Australian town, José stumbled upon a local writers' group. What began as a casual interest soon grew into an unquenchable passion. The stories swirling in his mind took shape, and from that creative spark, Danny Monk, his first major character, was born—a mischievous, intriguing figure who captured the complexities José had observed throughout his life. Writing Danny's story was a revelation, and with that, José discovered a new calling.

Fast forward to today. José is not just a writer but a prolific storyteller, balancing multiple projects at once. He is deep into his seventh short story collection while simultaneously crafting his latest work—a crime novel slated for release in 2026. His books, filled with engaging characters and complex narratives, reflect a life rich with experiences, challenges, and triumphs.

Yet José's world is not confined to the keyboard and screen. Inspiration comes from everywhere, and one of his favourite pastimes is to wander the local mall, quietly observing people, noting quirks, behaviours, and snippets of conversation that might spark a new character or plot twist.

When he's not writing or gathering ideas, José immerses himself in literature, feeding his mind with the words of others.

Outside of his creative pursuits, José treasures the simple pleasures of life—particularly long walks with his wife, Miriam, through the scenic streets of Spring Farm. Their leisurely strolls are a cherished routine, moments of reflection where stories, memories, and dreams intertwine.

José's life is a tapestry woven from adversity, perseverance, and creativity. From the orphanage in Georgia to the financial districts of the world, and now to the quiet corners of Spring Farm, where stories are born, his journey is a testament to the resilience of the human spirit. And with each book he writes, José not only tells stories but also leaves behind pieces of himself, enriching the lives of readers across the globe.

Of course, your comments, and reviews are always welcome.

Please be sure you visit my website https://worldbookreviews.com.au/book-reviews/ and let me know what you thought of this anthology of short stories and poetry.

Good, bad, or indifferent, I welcome your honest opinion.

Thank you for your purchase!

José F. Nodar © 2026

Other books by José F. Nodar:

English

- Books, Pens & Larceny

- Mending Hearts at Crystal Cove

- A Love Finally Spoken

- The Ghost Detective's First Case

- The Universe Between Us

- The Time Bus

- SEX

- Stories to Share with My Partner Book 1

- Stories to Share with My Partner Book 2

- Stories to Share with My Partner Book 3

- Stories to Share with My Partner Book 4

- Stories to Share with My Partner Book 5

- Stories to Share with My Partner Book 6

- Stories to Share with My Partner Book 7

Spanish

- Cuentos Para Compartir con Mi Pareja Libro 1

- Cuentos Para Compartir con Mi Pareja Libro 2

- Cuentos Para Compartir con Mi Pareja Libro 3

- Libros, Bolígrafos y Hurto

- Reparando Corazones en Crystal Cove

- Un Amor Expresado

- El Autobús del Tiempo